Wakefield Press

a new name for the colour blue

Dr Annette Marner is an award-winning poet, novelist, fine art nature photographer and ABC radio broadcaster from South Australia's Southern Flinders Ranges. In 2018, she won the Arts South Australia Wakefield Press Unpublished Manuscript Award at the Adelaide Festival Awards for Literature for *A New Name for the Colour Blue*. Her first book, *Women with Their Faces on Fire*, won the Unpublished Manuscript Award for Poetry for Friendly Street/Wakefield Press and was on the reading list at Flinders University.

Since launching her fine art nature photography in 2017, Annette has exhibited her work in galleries including solo exhibitions and had her images published internationally. Annette is an Associate Member of the Royal South Australian Society for Arts (qualifying in 2019 for her photography) and has a PhD in creative writing from Flinders University.

You can find Annette at annettemarner.com.

By the same author

Women with Their Faces on Fire

a
new
name
for the
colour
blue

Annette Marner

**Wakefield
Press**

Wakefield Press
16 Rose Street
Mile End
South Australia 5031
www.wakefieldpress.com.au

First published 2020

Cover designed by Annette Marner
Edited by Margot Lloyd, Wakefield Press
Typeset by Michael Deves, Wakefield Press

ISBN 978 1 74305 701 8

A catalogue record for this
book is available from the
National Library of Australia

Government
of South Australia

Department of the
Premier and Cabinet

CORIOLE

McLAREN VALE

Wakefield Press thanks
Coriole Vineyards for
continued support

For Kaz

Contents

The fugitive colours do less injury in the shadows than in the lights of a picture, because they are employed pure, and in greater body in shadows, and are therefore less liable to decay by the action of light, and by mixture.

George Field, *Field's Chromatography or Treatise on Colours and Pigments Used by Artists* (1841)

—— CHAPTER ONE ——

The Sorrows of the King

From the Brompton train, I can see galahs. After the last stop before the city, I put down my newspaper and press my face against the window of the train to look past the names cut into the glass and the white smears of city grime. On the clipped gardens between the groves of eucalyptus and the railway line galahs come to feed, their bodies like pink and grey shells scattered on the grass. I imagine I can hear them, but I know I can't above the sound of the train. I know they can't hear me, but sometimes when I remember what I have done I say it anyway, just in case: 'I'm sorry,' as if it were a prayer.

Adelaide is a city made of squares. Between the Mount Lofty Ranges and the sea, the streets are set at right angles as if the high church elders had laid down their crosses on the ground. The City of Churches. Planned within an inch of its life. So people would always know where they were going. So people couldn't get lost.

I walk across Victoria Square where Kaurna people sit in their circles on the grass while the buses and cars roar by us all, and the scent of diesel fills the air. The statue of the smug queen looks into the space above our heads as we pass by on our way to the grey honeycombs of the office blocks. Sometimes I think she has put something in the water to stop us growing wings. A homeless boy sleeps in the shadow of her plinth. This is Adelaide. My city of hope.

I catch the lift to my office in the community arts department. I say hello to my boss Vivienne, and sit down at my desk next to an Alexander palm in a rectangular pot made of varnished wood. I notice tiny balls of coloured paper lying on top of the bark chips in the pot. Wrappers from caramel lollies. As if someone were careless and dropped them there without thinking. It could have been me. I have a calendar on the wall of the art exhibitions I am organising in the city. None of them are mine.

I catch the 5.40 pm train to Tower Court. I go home to a townhouse in one of the new developments near the city where there is a garden the size of a table with a monstera plant growing in a bed of raised bricks. Where the sun can't touch you and give you ideas about perspective and colour. Inside my house, there are built-in cupboards made of chipboard. When you open the doors they smell of formaldehyde, as if they're painted with a kind of enamel that will never dry.

On the back of the bathroom door there is a long mirror. I have tried to take it down, but I'm afraid of breaking it so I leave the exhaust fan off when I'm in the shower to fill the bathroom with steam. Then, I can't see the body in the mirror. The one that belongs to me. If I can't see it, I can't hate it. I can't accuse it of its crimes against me: for lusting after men and sometimes women who do not care for me. For sometimes bringing them home anyway.

The water of the Ippinitchie River is the only mirror I have loved.

On the fridge door, I have a postcard of Van Gogh's *Vase with*

Twelve Sunflowers. He painted it in 1889. In Van Gogh's original, the colourants in the sunflowers are fugitive, vulnerable just like stories. They change and even disappear with time and light. I have my postcard where I can see it, not to remind me of the hardship of the artist's journey, but for the chrome yellow of the flowers. I need to be able to see it every day. To breathe it in. I think the colour must represent an absence in my life. But I don't know which one.

Above my bed, there is a picture of an Aboriginal girl with a skipping rope over her shoulder. The whole drawing is done with charcoal except for a flash of red crayon for the handles of the skipping rope. It isn't artist charcoal. It is charcoal I stole from the fireplace in the sitting room when Dad wasn't looking. The crayon came from school, and for the paper, I tore out a whole page from Mickey's sketchbook when he and Brendan were at football practice. I remember pulling out the scraps of paper from the wire spiral of the sketchbook so he would never know a page was gone. On the picture, just below the skipping rope, I wrote her name and a date in blue biro so no one could ever rub it out: *Tania Pepper 22-5-1967.* That's not the day I created the picture. That came a few weeks later. 22-5-1967 was the last day I saw her before she disappeared. It was the first drawing I ever did of someone I loved. I know I should move it to another wall. Away from the light.

I still see her sometimes in my sleep. She is walking through the blue and orange lights of the city or in the desert country of red ground, spinifex and oaks. Last night I dreamed she was climbing a green and blue mountain, the kind you see in the tropics, rich and heavy with steam and rain. She is still only a girl in my dreams, but that's how I remember her. In every dream she is walking. In every dream I call out her name. *Tania.*

In the hallway just inside the door, I've hung a giant print of *The*

Sorrows of the King by Matisse. In the middle of the image, there's a yellow guitar and two hands, white and disembodied, surrounded by black, magenta and green. A self-portrait. The artist who can no longer create. Matisse painted it in 1952, two years before he died. He knew the end was nigh. I hung it there when I stopped teaching art. When I stopped painting. When I stopped.

I still have dreams. But not the ones I used to have when I first came to the city from the Southern Flinders. Where you hope for something more. Where you hope at all.

———

A heavy blue light hangs over the garden in Jasper Street. It is not sky, but air that is clipped and pressed. Crisp waiters offer us champagne, smoked oysters and pâtés of quail, while above us moths are spiralling in their silvery paths like clouds of moving stars. I am dressed in pressed-linen white, and I have the taste of quince in my mouth when I hear him in the garden. In the light and shadows of the lamps, he is standing by the statue of Ajax, the sound of his saxophone crystal and blue across the white roses and the lawns. People have gathered around him, listening and watching, their faces angled and sleek with money.

I tap Hillary's shoulder.

'Not sure about his name,' she says, 'but I am sure what I'd do with him if I had the chance.'

Vivienne says, 'It's Stephen Chevalier from City of Searches, the Schurmanns' new band. Apparently, they came up with the name because in Adelaide we're always looking for children who have disappeared.'

I remember Dad saying to us whenever we went to Adelaide,

'Don't you three go wandering off. I don't want you ending up like the Beaumont children.' And Tania Pepper? Is anyone still searching for her? Is anyone out there still remembering and still grieving for her?

The saxophone of Stephen Chevalier wails and cries. Now reaching down to the great caverns of human loneliness. Now higher and deeper into the mysteries of the heart in space and time, where light and dark shimmer in the dance of being and not-being. His head falls back like Bernini's *Saint Teresa in Ecstasy*, as if his soul, like hers, is being pierced by a spear tipped with fire. A wave of warm sound passes through me. If it were light, it would have the glow of candles. Thousands of candles. As I listen, I imagine him with me naked in my bed. His mouth over my breasts, his body opening my thighs.

By the time he finishes playing, I know he has chosen me.

I park my car under the plane tree by my house. I'm trying to be cool, but by the time I reach the door, I can hardly breathe. I drop the keys. He picks them up and hands them to me. Between the hallstand and the print of Matisse, we are nothing but pulse and breath and skin.

At a quarter past ten on Sunday night, he leaves. I don't want to sleep. I want to remember everything over and over. Every cry and every kiss. So I stay awake until dawn. But I have to go to work. I have to meet Hillary for breakfast. I have to wash him off me.

Il Vero Café is still quiet when I arrive, because it's too early even for the politicians and lawyers with their black suits and earnest faces. The leaves are turning and starting to fall. Grey clouds cross the shaft of the city sky from north to south like corrugated iron end to end. On some days, such a sky reminds me of looking up at the iron verandah at Ippinitchie River. But in this minute, I have no heart for that particular sorrow. For now, I have silence to remember the scent of him and the taste of him on my tongue. Hillary lights a cigarette and studies my face over the gold rims of her sunglasses.

'Christ, Cassandra, look at you. Just be certain he's what you want.'

'How can you tell?'

'Fuck him for a while and see.'

'You're so bloody mercenary,' I say.

A laugh starts in my chest and rushes upwards, but the sound is squeezed somewhere in my throat. I put my hand there to help it come out. It doesn't.

———

Our thighs kiss as we walk in step along the beach wrapped in his overcoat. I feel his open hand on my hip holding on. As if I were something precious he was afraid of losing. Around us is the noise of the waves shattering like grey glass on the sand, and the cry of the Caspian terns as they hunt across the water. This is an autumn evening on a deserted Carrickalinga beach. A blue line splits the sea and sky as the storm comes, and the light in the west burns into silver sheets of lightning. He takes my hand in the rain and we run back to our cabin. We have a shower so hot and long, the water almost hurts. The thunder shakes the ceiling and the lights go out.

He carries me to the bed and presses himself into me.

I lie against his chest, the storm and rain beating around us.

He says, 'Lightning is static electricity with attitude.'

'Static can mean unchanging too,' I say.

I say it because I want us to be that way. I was taught at school that things in the universe were fixed. The position of stars. The distances between galaxies. I want us to be like the universe used to be in our minds. Unchanging. Even if we were wrong.

I do not recognise this body in the bathroom mirror, as I count the places he has kissed.

If stars can bend time and space, can they also bend memory? Two weeks have gone by, and I have not thought once to dust the picture of Tania.

I say in a whisper to her, 'Soon. Soon.'

The wine glasses of Molly and Keith Schurmann do not match, and there is a jumble of wattle flowers scattered across their table. The dining chairs are an assortment of spindle backs from the early 1900s. Aunty Nell and Cousin Teddie had chairs just like these in the kitchen at Ippinitchie River, but each one of these chairs is painted in a primary colour, and there are spaces where the bare wood shows through in smears rounded and dark like the rich clouds of autumn. I don't know if the chairs were painted carelessly or if the effect was deliberate. Perhaps it is neither. Perhaps the paint has worn away from years of touch from all the people who have dined here. As I look around this table I feel a hunger rise inside me. Not for food or something sweet. Not for sex or chocolate. I don't know what I hunger for.

I remember the untidiness of rivers.

The water in the deep pools of the Ippinitchie shimmered in summer, the colour of tar. Close by the banks, the tender awns of the kangaroo grass were angled and hung in the wind as if they were broken. But the longer I stayed listening and watching, the more it seemed each river stone was in its right place; each fallen limb, as it lay awkwardly across the bank, was meant to be there, and each awn of the kangaroo grass whispered to me of home.

Molly says, 'The energy of every musical note as it's played moves through space like a wave. It is pure energy and it's powerful and beautiful. Energy influences matter.'

I smile at the pure wonder of it. I say, 'Music can influence matter? Can it really do that?'

'Oh yes,' Stephen says. 'We've known that for centuries.' I am suddenly aware of his hand open and firm on my thigh. He turns to me. 'That's the physics of music I was telling you about. Don't you remember?'

I must have forgotten so I trust his memory over mine. A blush lights up my face, and I feel the heat move like hot oil up my neck and across my cheeks.

Keith offers me wine and says, 'The *viola d'amore* from the baroque had two sets of matching strings, but the musician only played one set. The other resonated without being touched.'

I look at Stephen. I will tell him later that now I know why my body hums when he's not even with me.

Molly says, 'Would you like to see the house?'

Keith smiles and says, 'What she really means is, "Would you like to see the artworks?" She loves to show them off.'

On the lounge room wall there are originals by Pro Hart and Margaret Olley, and by the top of the stairs a print of a Leonardo da Vinci painting called *Scapigliata*. The woman in the painting looks like a photograph of a sculpture. Layer upon layer of depth as if you could reach in and touch her brow of stone.

I say, 'Why does anyone bother to paint in the wake of the Maestro? He achieved perfection.'

Molly slips her arm into mine, and leads me to the other side of the landing. On the wall above me, there is an oil painting of the ruin of a little cottage. She-oaks grow through the broken roof and walls. Their golden flowers tumble across the stone. In the corner of the painting, barbed wire encircles a single red geranium. The painting is called *Sarah's Garden*.

Molly says, 'She doesn't need to paint like da Vinci. The world needs her to paint like this.'

I see my name in blue ink at the bottom of the painting. It feels like a photo of my childhood: I know it's me, but it's a life I can't possibly remember.

'We waited for your solo exhibition, but it never came.'

'No,' I say.

I drive us back to the city. His fingers stroke my neck as we descend from the dark hills to the frieze of white lights below. Each light is a home. As if a home and family is not a rare and precious thing, but ordinary and abundant like she-oaks. Like galahs.

'You never told me you could paint like that.'

'Because I can't. Not anymore.'

His hand on my neck shape-shifts into a fist. He brushes my cheek with his knuckles.

'You should have told me, Cassandra,' he says. 'You made me look like a fool in front of my friends.'

A moth explodes as it hits the windscreen. I switch on my wipers. For a moment, I cannot see where I am going.

'I'm really sorry, Stephen.'

We descend to where the orange streetlights at the intersections

9

hollow out the darkness. I can no longer tell if my headlights are on, can no longer see their long white funnels opening up the faces of the trees. The city opens up like a mouth and swallows us whole.

———

Hillary and I are beyond the dirty mud-holes of power. We see the black suits networking around us, gossiping and positioning, and we laugh to ourselves quietly. They are the bat people in their dark folds and padded shoulders. We are the elite. We work on the ground. Where it matters. Where the art is made.

I am a moth trapped inside a white cup.

The training room is fluorescent white. Walls, ceilings, even the tables and chairs are dazzling, but there is no real light. The heavy pink vertical blinds over the windows are shut tight like eyelids that don't want to open.

The trainer gives us a sheet with just one sentence typed on it:

FABULOUS FILMS ARE THE RESULT
OF YEARS OF FANCY FOOTWORK WITH FINANCIERS
AND THE EFFORT OF MANY PEOPLE

We have sixty seconds to find each letter *F* within the sentence. I put my index finger under the first word and start to count. I write my answer in a box at the bottom of the page.

The trainer asks, 'How many see seven?'

I raise my hand. Hillary is sitting across from me looking down at her sheet. I can't read her face, but I know whatever she is going to say now will be wrong.

The trainer says, 'So tell me, who has counted ten?'

Hillary raises her hand. I flip the sheet over thinking it must be a "think outside the square" kind of trick. The sheet is blank. The trainer moves towards her.

He glances at her nametag, 'Hillary, that's well done. Excellent. Now the rest of you no doubt are very confused, but let me assure you there is no trick here. There is only the blinding power of your mindsets. Your beliefs, not your objective senses, interpret the world for you. And in this case, your mindsets' interpretation of the world is wrong.' He turns on the overhead projector.

'"Fabulous films are the result ..." Here you counted two, and you are correct. 'But how many are in the second line: "Of years of fancy footwork with financiers". Three or five?'

'Christ,' says a voice behind me, 'there are five.'

'Have the rest of you worked it out yet?' The trainer asks.

We nod. Some of us are lying.

'The simple answer,' says the trainer, 'is that our eyes see, but our brains, our mindsets, interpret what our eyes are seeing. The letter *F* in the word *of* registers in our brains as a *V*, because that's how it sounds when we read the sentence. We do not count it, because we do not see it. The phenomenon is called *scotoma*.'

I'd checked each letter so carefully. I was so certain. I don't know what to trust if not my eyes. What else am I *not* seeing? Or is this worse: what am I seeing *incorrectly*?

———

It is late autumn and the plane trees have shed their leaves at Tower Court. By my front gate the leaves are ankle deep. I don't rake them up or sweep them away. I like the feeling of kicking my way through them, giving them motion and air. Outside, I am flanked by the cold south-westerly coming in from the sea. All that cement and iron and bitumen between the coast and here is not enough to warm the wind.

Stephen and I are awake late into the night. I cook pasta at midnight when our bodies are tired after love. When he can't sleep at 2.00 am, I make him lemon tea. Every morning, I have to run hard for the train. And I forget things. My briefcase. To pay the electricity bill. How I was before I met him.

I change colours when he looks at me. If I could still paint, I would paint a naked female body with ley lines of ecstasy crossing over swollen lips, vulva and breasts, in waves of rose dorée, violet and cerulean blue. And I would paint her eyes shining like the Ippinitchie River after the second of the winter rains when the water moves dustless and clear over the black branches and the stones.

How do you escape the geography of a life? He wants me to go to Wilpena with him. He says he wants to feel the ancient energy of the Flinders Ranges at Brachina and Bunyeroo Valley to inspire the next album. When we drive northwards on the highway, will the great blue wall of the Flinders mountains be high enough to separate me from the landscapes of my childhood? Could memories cross over such a wall? Will I be able to stop myself from imagining my father tending his bean rows on the other side of the mountains? And how, every now and then, he will stop to rest, his forearms leaning against the handle of his garden fork. He will look into the distance reading the sky for rain or the south-westerly change. And he won't be unhappy. He prefers everything to be at a distance: the memory of my mother and Tania. And me.

From Hope Gap to Winninowie, on the plains of northern Spencer Gulf, I look only westwards through the red mallee and pearl bluebush to the sea. We cross over creeks and rivers, empty and still, and the outwash fans cut into the footslopes of the Southern Flinders like broad wounds that have dried, but have not healed. I do not look eastwards to the mountains of my childhood. We play Stan Getz in the car with the volume up so loud I can't hear myself think. I don't want to think. Thinking might slip into remembering.

The memory of water is long. Half a billion years have passed, but the shape of moving waves is still here, imprinted onto Flinders Ranges stone. Everywhere I look, there are miracles of life on the Brachina escarpments. On ledges no wider than my hand, porcupine grass and she-oaks grow out of invisible earth. We follow a narrow path by the creek surrounded by low hills and red gum saplings. Stephen leads carrying his saxophone. As we walk, the low hills quietly transform into massive cliffs of broken sandstone and deep green native pine, their cones opening into petals, rust-coloured and hard. I carry a single cone for a while, just to feel it in my fingers, but then I let it go. I used to think that history laid down its truths one after another like layer upon layer of coloured sand. But here, in these towering mountains, I see how time and pressure distort the strata of history. The tectonics of time. The uplift from the deep earth, and the scouring by water and wind can tilt even a mountain from its axis.

The air cools as the sunlight disappears, but that is not the reason I feel a shiver crack across my body. I look up at those powerful cliffs. On the tip of the escarpment, the long afternoon sun flickers and disappears in a scree of golden dust. Now only the highest peaks to our right are sunlit. There the limbs of the Flinders Ranges box trees gleam copper against the red orange of the rock. This gorge is a mansion and we are the guests who have entered the dark wing uninvited.

I say to Stephen in a whisper, 'This feels like such a sacred place. I want to ask for permission.'

'For what, exactly?'

'To be here.'

He snaps the latches of his case and takes out his saxophone. A flock of parrots rises from the she-oaks in green and yellow fire.

'That's not what I meant,' I laugh. But I hear the false notes in my throat, clipped and hard.

The reed in his mouth trembles against his breath. Soundwaves cross the air. I hear them curl and break against the walls of rock before coming back to us, a reflected pulse, sharp and brazen. After the last notes are played, I can't be certain if the sound weakens or if it's moving further away, but it grows softer until it's gone. I don't know where soundwaves go when they're reflected off stone. Maybe they charge into the deep of things: bark, grass, feathers, and change what's there. I know soundwaves can change things. The sound of a single sentence can alter a life, sentences like *I love you Cassandra*.

'Hey man,' says a voice calling above us, 'that was brilliant.' Two young hikers clap their hands and wave at us from the path along the mountainside. 'Never thought we'd get to hear a cool sax like that out here,' the hiker yells. 'Hey, what's your name?'

'Stephen Chevalier.'

The hiker turns to his companion and slaps him on the shoulder, and calls out to us, 'I knew it. I heard you play at the Gov last week. My mate here didn't believe it was you. You've just won me a dozen beers. Thanks for the free show.'

Stephen bows to them, and looks at me, 'Is that enough permission for you?'

He picks a flower from a rocky ledge, a lilac isotome, and tucks it behind my ear. I don't want to tell him that the white sap from the stem, already damp in my hair, is poison to the eyes.

Later, by the dark thigh of a river red gum, he touches me softly. Our bodies are white and trembling against the silent grass. I say to myself *remember this*: the sweet scent of him, and the stars, a crown in the curls of his hair.

I press the isotome between the pages of Yeats's *Collected Poems*. Its five petals are purple ink brushed across the page.

At dinner he gives me a ring. It is blue opal flecked with crimson and green. He holds it against the candlelight.

'It has waited in the desert for you for twenty-five million years.' His hands press hard, a *V* against my cheeks. 'I promise I'll always look after you. You're my family. You're mine.'

I kiss him across the table until I feel the candle flame against my skin, a breath from burning.

I phone Hillary to tell her about the ring.

I say, 'I feel like I'm the one who has been in the desert waiting for him for twenty-five million years. And now he's found me.'

I make space for him. I sell the hallstand to the second-hand dealer on Port Road. I clean out the bathroom cupboard. I make room for his aftershave, and the soap that makes him smell like wood. He will take away the scent of formaldehyde.

I run home from the train. As I approach the front gate, I hear Guns N' Roses singing 'Sweet Child O' Mine'. He's here. His saxophones will be in the hallway. His tailored jackets and white shirts will be in the bedroom, his razor in the bathroom. I drop my keys at the door. I can smell ginger. He is in the kitchen cooking vindaloo. I slip my hands around his neck and he kisses me hard against the pantry door. The air is spiced, hot like cayenne. He says, 'How was your day?'

'It was great,' I lie. But sometimes you have to do that to be happy.

I have to work late. Again. I miss the 6.35 pm train. I phone Stephen at Tower Court, but he doesn't answer. I run from the train station in my high heels carrying my briefcase and umbrella. The city smells of frangipani. Rain and city lights are an orange wash across the streets. By the time I reach the door I can hardly breathe. I drop the keys. He is on the couch reading the newspaper so I can't see his face.

I say, 'I'm sorry I'm late,' and move closer to kiss him. He drops the newspaper and asks me where I've been. He sniffs at me. I ask him what he's doing.

'Seeing if another man has fucked you.'

'What do you mean? I was late. That's all. I tried to call.'

'No, no, no.' The tightness in his face squeezes the words until they are so narrow they are no longer language. They could be just howls. 'No, not good enough.' He kicks over the glass coffee table. Pizza slices from his takeaway dinner land upside down on the carpet.

I drop to my hands and knees and start to pick them up.

'Don't worry, I'll fix it,' I say. The cheese is greasy and keeps sticking to the carpet while under my knees, I can feel the oil from the anchovies seeping into my suit trousers.

'Well you're responsible for the fucking mess, aren't you?'

I want to speak. But I have no words. My language has collapsed in on itself like the core of a dying star. Through the shockwaves, nothing can escape. No sound. No light. He leans down next to my ear, 'Fucking answer me.'

But I am a black hole. I am no size.

He takes the keys to my car and slams the front door behind him. I clean the carpet. I eat toast for dinner but it hurts each time I swallow. I don't know what to do. Vivienne is picking me up in her work car at seven o'clock in the morning to drive us to a meeting at Semaphore. She will expect me to be here. I have to be here. I get into bed with my clothes on. The air in the room is thick, like the scent of anchovies.

I hear my car outside. It's 3.20 am. He comes into the bedroom and whispers to me in the dark, 'Come here my darling girl. Let's not fight.'

I didn't know I was fighting.

I hurt, from him. He comforts me. Such is love. He turns on the lamp. When he is about to kiss me again, I see something I have never noticed before. A small white scar on his lip in the shape of a scythe.

Where does light go when it's turned off?

He says I can help him heal. From the drunken beltings his mother gave him when he was little. He says no one else has been able to get close like I can. When he says that, I think I am meant to feel love or pity. What I feel is responsibility.

I see myself in the mirror of his saxophone. I am all nose and small dark eyes. Everything about me is wrong. *Ugly and wrong.* When I started school at Ippinitchie River, that's what the other children told me. Except Tania. I stand on the bed and polish the glass that protects my drawing of her from silverfish, from dust, from forgetfulness.

CHAPTER TWO

Ajax and Cassandra

The sky here in the city is all geometry. Rectangles of sky shine between the crests of the high rise, sharp-angled and long. Inside the atrium of the Adelaide Central Market, I look up and see a grey square. It could be cement. It could be sky.

The rich scents of coffee and roasted tomatoes hover in the air at Lucia's café. At my favourite table in the corner, Stephen kisses me and gives me a book on Degas. He says I just need to learn what upsets him. That's all. Then we'll be fine. He says he loves me. He says he can't wait to see me tonight. Under the table, he has his hand on my knee. What I feel is gratitude.

The first light of morning through the window in the hallway is the colour of hay. The light falls on to the frame of the Matisse. I am in the kitchen with a black coffee and the noise of the New Holland honeyeaters waking in the garden. I hold the coffee cup to my cheek. It is the temperature now of his face when he's loving me. And he does love me. He does.

I don't want the life I had. The dark hollows after work with no one to discuss the day. No one to cook for. No sex except with strangers. No arms around me while I sleep. But how do we rebuild? Heinrich Schliemann, a German amateur scholar, spent years studying Homer's descriptions of Troy in *The Iliad*, and decided Troy must be in north-west Turkey on the site of Hissarlik. In 1873, he found it deep below other ruins, the strata of other destroyed cities. On the same ground, over and over, they planned, they built and they destroyed. The ground of suffering. The ground of memory. Stephen, we must forgive each other for the stones upon which we break.

Sunday afternoon at Tower Court and the sun doesn't reach the window. He asks me to read Yeats to him.

I say, 'I need to go over some work papers for tomorrow. Can we do it later?'

'Jesus fucking Christ! You never give me what I want.' He hits me on the thigh, not hard enough to bruise. Just hard enough to hurt.

I thought I had a line in my head that said, *If he crosses this, I'll leave.* But the line is a mirage on the road. It melts, and shifts, then reappears again, shimmering and blinding, so you can never know exactly where it is. All you know is you get there and it's gone.

I am crusted with salt. I walk along the jetty at Semaphore Beach expecting freshness, newness, but the air is thick with the smell of rotting sea grass. I am not looking up enough today. I am seeing too much of the ground. And it feels soiled. Stale from the scattered leaves from the afternoon tide, a cigarette butt still smoking like a fuse, spat from a teenage boy in jeans that canopy his shoes. I walk in the path of a thousand footprints. I want to tell someone, ask someone, but with every step in the wet sand I hear the word *hush*.

I buy hot chips. The silver gulls come in and enclose me on the sand. One takes the centre ground in front of me. It lowers its head like a bull and charges at the others to keep them away. I don't know if this boss bird is male or female. Perhaps it doesn't matter. I remind myself it's just natural selection at work, rewarding the strong and the self-absorbed. Beyond the white circle, one gull balances on a single leg in the wind. I wonder if it was trapped in fishing line, or if, one day when it was resting on the comfortable water, a fish came along and bit off its leg, out of hunger, boredom or spite.

The wind comes in the night and wakes us. Later it is quiet, but the darkness stays.

Stephen says, 'You're harder than you used to be. When we first met you were softer.'

I feel something rise up inside me. I have to swallow hard to make it go back down. Rage. Or sadness. I can't tell which. I put my fingers into my mouth, so whatever it is can't get out.

I dream Stephen is a giant dragonfly who has laid eggs in my brain. I can see the yellow hatchlings crawling on my fingers. They look like maggots. I'm being colonised.

He doesn't like the way I boil the kettle. He says the automatic switch is too slow. He wants me to stand in the kitchen and wait for it to boil so the water for his lemon tea isn't stale.

I say, 'I don't want to stand in the kitchen waiting for the kettle.'

He says, 'Do you know how hard it is for me living in this house? Your house. Every fucking thing is yours whether I like it or not. Like that fucking picture in the bedroom of that black girl. It says fuck all to me, but I have to live with it, because it's Cassandra's. It's fucking Cassandra's.' He picks up the kettle, 'It's a fucking ugly fucking thing like this fucking ugly, useless fucking kettle.' He smashes it against the door. 'Now we need a new one,' he says.

I stay up late until he is asleep on the lounge. I take down my picture of Tania Pepper and slip it into my briefcase. I take it to work and hide it in my desk drawer. At lunch I go to the butcher in the Central Market. I buy two organic pork steaks and a Granny Smith apple. I catch the train. I drop my keys at the front door. He is not here. I wait for something to happen.

The light from the garden is soft so the shadow of my hand against the page I'm reading is abstract. I cannot tell where it ends, or if I'm disappearing and I can't cast shadows anymore. I eat pink and black licorice allsorts, two at a time until my teeth ache and my arms go red and I start to scratch. My jeans feel tight so I have to loosen my belt. I put the phone next to my bed so the ring will wake me in the night. I stare at it. He might call. He might be desperate. He might be sorry.

He phones me at midnight. He says he would never want to cause me any pain. He says he wants me to try harder. I tell him I will. He says he doesn't want Hillary coming over for dinner next week. I say okay.

My voice is light and full of air like foam. Not like the foam that gathers at the bend in a river. The sort that is made of plastic or petrol. The sort that is artificial. Produced.

I say to Hillary, 'I have to cancel next week.'

'Christ, Cassandra. I haven't even been to your place since he moved in. Are you still fucking each other's brains out?'

I try to generate a laugh. I can't.

I wait. Because I need to get stronger so I can leave him. I'll know what to do when I'm stronger.

I get bars put on the windows and deadlocks on the doors to keep out home invaders. The city is going into lockdown. Along my street, people are putting roll-up metal blinds on the outside of the windows to keep out intruders. When Stephen is out at night, I listen to talkback radio so I'm less afraid. And I listen because I want to hear people's stories about their stolen cars, graffiti on their fences, the banks increasing interest rates again. I need to hear their anger, so I can get angry for them. I know how to do that. Get angry for someone else.

Today I made a plan. I put it in a red envelope at work next to Tania's picture, so he can't see it. The plan isn't finished. This is what I have so far:

When I ask him to leave, he will go into a rage. I can't predict what might happen then. He might break something I value. He knows what those things are. He might hurt me. I don't want anyone I know to see him in a rage against me. I can't put them through that. Therefore, I have to escape from him on my own.

How do I get him and his things out of my house?

1. Wait until he is away for the weekend. (So I can't be working and or have any engagements – no birthdays, etc. If I cancel in advance he'll find out and wonder why.)

2. *Pack up his things in boxes.*

3. *Deliver the boxes of his things, but to where? (His music, his saxophones – I can't just leave everything on the street. I don't have the money to replace them if they're stolen, and I can't send them to Keith and Molly's. That would be involving them and he's their friend.)*

4. *Change the lock on the front door, but I have to manage the timing. It has to be a weekend when he's away. I need to find out if locksmiths work on weekends. What if the locksmith comes when I am not there and Stephen is because his gig is cancelled?*

5. *I can't be there when he gets back.*

6. *Do I leave a note for him saying it's over? How do I tell him?*

After I leave:

Stephen must not be able to contact me. So:

1. I turn off my phone.

2. I get a new number.

What if work wants me? What number do I give? I have to be contactable. He knows where I work. He has my work number. Do I tell work not to transfer his calls to me? Then they'll know. Then he'll just pretend he's someone else. He can do that. He knows names. And he will tell the people at work how flawed I am. He knows a lot of people. He knows Vivienne. And he knows the patterns of my life. My places. Il Vero Café on North Terrace. Lucia's in the Central Market. So I will have to eat at different places. And I'll have to catch different trains. He could turn up anywhere. He will want to. He will want to say something to me. He will want to do something. I don't know how to stop that.

So, I need to go away for a while where he can't find me. How can I do that? What about work? I only have three days accrued holidays. I've used my leave when Stephen is away to go to Carrickalinga. To heal. To recover. Do I take leave without pay? Will work let me have it? Vivienne will want to know why I want the leave. I can't tell her. She'll use it against me. I don't have enough money to take leave without pay anyway. I have to save up so I can leave him.

'You look like crap,' Hillary says over lunch. She wipes the carbonara sauce from her mouth. 'So, is it too much work or too little sex? It has to be one or the other.' She grins over her raised glass of riesling.

I want to tell someone. But once I say it, everything will change and I don't know what might happen, what might be let loose. I want to say that living with Stephen is like breathing in splinters of barbed wire. And that I want her help to get me out. To save me. But once I speak, my dream is dead. I want Carrickalinga beach during the thunderstorm. I want his heartbeat on my cheek. If I speak now, there is no hope I can ever have that again. There's no going back. Not ever.

What I say to her is, 'He's not easy sometimes, Hillary.'

She pushes back against her chair and laughs. 'He's a musician. What did you expect? Someone who'd play golf on Sundays and balance his chequebook every second week? He's not that kind of man. Christ, hand him over to me. I'll sort him out for you.'

I ask, 'What would you do?'

'You really want to know?'

'Yes.'

'I'd fuck him till he couldn't walk.'

He cooks me puttanesca. We watch *Dead Calm*. He puts his hands over my eyes during the scary bits. This makes me laugh. My body loosens into him. He touches me as if I'm healing him. As if he's healing me.

He turns off the bed lamp and leans over me.

'Sometimes, I'm a cunt of a man to you, a cunt of a man. You bring it out in me. I want you to stop bringing it out in me.'

'How do you know it's me?'

'Because I've never been like that with anyone else.' He kisses me on the ear. 'You've never lived with anyone before, but I can teach you.'

'I want to sleep, Stephen.' But he is already lying across me, holding me.

'You promised you would try harder, remember? You're not.'

'I want to sleep. Please.'

'Shush,' he says. He turns my head so his mouth can reach me. Between my thighs I burn, a hot iron-against-my-skin burn. There is nowhere to go. This is meant to be home: him and me together in this bed. If this is home, I don't understand why I want to be absent. How I can be absent.

I sit down on the floor with my back to the chair thinking about the word *ravished*. It's such an explosive word. It can mean *rape* and it can mean *enrapture, filled with delight*. How can a single word mean such opposites?

He sleeps on his side turned towards me. It is a deep and confident sleep. His arm is across my waist, his hand open on my skin. Tonight some things are different. On my bedside table there are daffodils as bright as candles that he gave to me when I got home from work. Some of the feeling of him in my body has gone away. There is moonlight on the curtain. Everything else is the same.

I press a towel into the bruises. And in the shower, I let the warm water pour down my breasts and belly, washing him off. Away.

The pain of him is blue, the colour of the horizon in summer, heavy with dust and heat, dragged down to the edges of the world. This is how we live now. He chastises me, calls me names. I go out. I miss him. So I come home, afraid he won't be there. And afraid he will be there. I'm noticing a new habit. I roll my lips inwards whenever I get angry. This means I cannot pronounce words, just sounds with different pitches, but I don't let them out either. I just let them sound in my head.

He flies me to Melbourne for my birthday. He takes me to the National Gallery.

'I thought it might inspire you to take up painting again,' he says.

I am standing in front of Clara Southern's *An Old Bee Farm* that she painted in 1900. A woman tends her bees. She wears a long skirt with a purple-blue apron wrapped about her waist. We can't see her face. She is in a clearing with her cottage behind her. The colours of her apron and the surrounding bushland call softly to each other. She is a woman alone in the Australian landscape but neither lonely, lost nor afraid.

My eyes fill with tears. I want to howl. This is the closest I have come to crying.

'My sensitive little artiste,' he says. 'What would you do without me?'

I say, 'I don't know, Stephen.' And that is a truth that is absolute.

In the dark, he says, 'I'm not sure you are what I want.'

I say, 'Tell me what you want and I'll be that.'

I have to check the stove is off. I look at the switch and spell out the letters like a child does when spelling a new word for the first time. I say the letters out loud, 'O-F-F', but I can't believe or trust what I am saying.

'Hurry up!' Stephen yells from the front door.

'I just have to do something.'

I look again at the switch. I touch it and say, 'O-F-F'. But I still can't believe it. So I splay my right hand across the burner. Now I believe it because no pain comes.

He says he doesn't like Hillary. He says he doesn't want me to have lunch with her anymore if I can have lunch with him instead. I say okay.

I dream swords are sticking out from all the walls. The blades are close together like echidna spines, but long and sharp and gleaming in the half-light. They could be the sort magicians use to pierce a cabinet with a woman inside. And it is always a woman inside. Always. I know if I can stay small the blades won't cut me, but my body is getting bigger. I inhale slowly, trying to tighten my chest to stop my rib cage expanding. I hold my breath, waiting in the dark, wondering what to do. Now the ceiling starts to slide down the walls. I wonder if the swords will kill me before I am crushed. As I breathe in, a blade bores into the left side of my chest towards my heart. I can't see the wound, but I can hear my blood falling to the floor.

I need a list now in the mornings so I can leave the house. So I know what to do. I've put the items in a column so there's room to tick them. I don't cross them out in case I make a mistake.

Light the stove
Put coffee in percolator
Add water
Cut grapefruit in half
Put grapefruit on plate
Add sugar
Pour coffee
Turn off stove
Check I've turned off stove
Have breakfast
Do dishes
Have shower
Turn off taps
Check taps are off
Put on make up
Get dressed
Pick up briefcase
Check stove is off
Lock front door
Lock security door
Pull on door (twice) to make certain it's locked

The language of my body is changing. Sitting in the chair, my right hand hangs on to my left shoulder and my fingers curl into the collar of my suit. It's the grip of a baby.

I am awake in the lonely dark thinking of the fall of Troy. In the temple to the goddess Athena, Cassandra is seized by Ajax. He, the warrior, the maker of war. She, the handmaiden, the virgin, and prophet of Troy. There is a painting of this moment by Solomon J. Solomon called *Ajax and Cassandra*. They are both naked except for the cloths draped across their thighs. His cloth is red. Hers is white, diaphanous and light. His right hand is coiled into a fist. He holds her over his left shoulder. Against his grip and pull, she is grasping the statue of the goddess with her fingers. You cannot see Cassandra's face. She is anatomy now. Thighs. Breasts. Cunt. The spoils of war. She is about to be destroyed. The temple burned. The flame put out. She is already the colour of death.

Dr Jayne Cotton's office has a tapestry called *Egret Climbing.* It hangs on the wall above the chesterfield and the Kentia palms. On the left hand side of the tapestry are the words, 'To rise, you must face the wind.'

She says, 'What was your childhood like?'

'It was a typical country childhood. Big skies, sport and lots of cakes. And it was Catholic, so millions of Hail Marys.'

'Your father?'

'The other day at the beach I watched a man with his daughter on his shoulders. She was laughing. She was safe. It made me feel like a failure. I just don't have memories like that.'

'Your father never gave you a piggyback?'

'No.'

'Kissed you goodnight?'

'No. Never.'

'How did you feel about that?'

'What was wrong with me, that he didn't want to be near me?'

'And your mother?'

'One day – I don't know how old I was, but it was before I started school. I remember it was sunny. I was on the verandah with Mum and Aunty Nell. Mum was brushing my hair. I tried to climb onto her lap like I'd done the week before, but she pinched me on the arm.'

'Why did she do that do you think?'

My body is shaking.

'Because she thought I wasn't a baby anymore. I shouldn't be mothered. I'd get spoilt.'

'But she hugged you sometimes?'

'No. She never hugged me again.'

'Did she touch you at all?'

'She touched me on Fridays. She'd warm the curling tongs on the stove and put Curly Pet lotion in my hair with her fingers. I remember her fingers were rough at the tips and scratched a little bit. When she turned back to the stove to get the tongs, I'd flatten a curl with my hand, so she'd have to do it again. And of course she touched me when she belted me. But she used a wooden spoon,' I laugh, 'so that's not really touching me, is it? And it only happened once. I said something I shouldn't have to our priest. I've forgotten what it was.'

'What comes into your mind when you think of her?'

'She put Dad and the boys first. Always. And they never seemed to care about how much work she did for them. Especially Dad. He never said, "Gee, I bet you had a tough time today cooking that roast in the middle of a heatwave." But she didn't know how to say thank you, either. When Cousin Teddie dropped off almonds he'd grown, or a leg of mutton if he'd killed a sheep, she'd just look awkward and small. She didn't know how to behave when someone gave her anything. She'd just pretend it hadn't happened.'

'It is interesting to postulate about other lives. To consider the

31

influence of the family, genetically and culturally, along with the influence of the place and year of someone's birth. What were they brought up to believe? What opportunities were available to them? What skills did they need to survive? I call these "the coordinates of a life: Blood. Geography. Time". They are a starting point to consider the differences in how people live their lives. I would like you to write down the things that were integral to your mother's life, but not yours. I think it will offer you new perspectives.

I open my notebook and begin to write:

These are the things my mother could do that I can't: milk a cow by hand, cry over the souls in purgatory, waltz, never miss Sunday Mass, assemble a milk separator, pray for the souls of unbaptised babies lost forever in Limbo, only go to primary school, use lard for cooking, remember to wind the mantel clock every Monday, not read books, wear rhinestones and roll-ons, pray the rosary every night by the Immaculate Heart of Mary, rely entirely on my spouse for money, believe what Father Michael said in the sermon, kill a snake with a wire, live without the pill, clean a rabbit, prop the clothesline against the wind, love Dad, die alone.

I say, 'This is a life I do not recognise.'

'Or want?' Dr Cotton asks.

'No. I would not want it.'

Dr Cotton says, 'I'd like you to look at your list for a couple of minutes every day during the next week. If you can do that, you will be affirming your new awareness of your mother's life.' She makes a note in the folder on her desk and says, 'Now, in this second part of our session today, I want you to think about anger. Do you ever feel angry, or display anger?'

'Often,' I say. 'I'm angry at poverty and tyranny.'

'And in your relationship with Stephen?'

'No. I don't get angry with Stephen.'

'Okay. What have you seen in the last month that's made you angry?'

I say, 'I went for a drive to a park called the Garden of Birds, thinking I'd have a sandwich in a quiet spot and watch the birds. But all the birds were in cages. Birds like kookaburras and honeyeaters that would have been in the garden anyway. In a clearing, two men were looking through a wire cage at a wedge-tailed eagle. They laughed at it, the way it was so clumsy on its feet, those giant legs, thick with feathers, the way it hung one wing on the ground, dragging it through the dirt like a torn cloak, around and around the cage. Then it stopped by me, and it's the first time I'd ever been so close to a wedge-tail. I saw its eyes looking at me like onyx and fire, its magnificent head, all noble and desperate, and I felt such shame. Then it stumbled on and fell in the dirt. It got up, bruised with dust, and started running and falling around the cage again.'

'Why did you feel shame rather than anger when you saw the eagle? You said that this was going to be a story about anger.'

'I don't know.' I sip from a glass of water. I replace it carefully on the coaster of her desk. I say, 'I know why the garden upset me. I'm not the eagle. Stephen is. He tells me all the time that I've caged him.'

'Who are you?'

'I must be the owner of the garden.'

I am wondering about the geography of my life. The Southern Flinders with its gentle-shaped mountains. And its sandstone barns and cottages that in the thick evening light turn to saffron and gold against the trees and fields of grain. How did this landscape change me? The grey box with its softness of pale blossoms in winter. And the last of the river red gum forest along the Ippinitchie that used to speak to me, but only in whispers?

Stephen is out partying or rehearsing, I don't know which, but I have some time alone. I sit on the couch with a science magazine, and it falls open at an article about quantum theory that says nothing can be observed and measured without being disturbed. So we change whatever it is we're watching. So, the eagle changed with the men and me watching it. And we were changed too. But in what way?

Do we disturb the dead when we try to pick apart the history of their lives?

I tear out the page from my notebook that I had written about my mother.

I dream it is necessary to reach into my chest and pull out my soul. I watch it flail slippery and wet in my hand like a fingerling. It has fins of silver that beat the air so fast they turn into a blur. I drop my soul into an airtight jar so it can't get away. As I press down on the lid I hear a sigh. I don't know if that's the sound of relief or protest. I place the jar on a shelf next to my mother's mantel clock and the picture of the Immaculate Heart of Mary. It is necessary to put my soul in a jar because in the natural laws of this dream world, it was about to leave me. A soul will do that. Leave a body. From too much pain or not enough.

———

Stephen looks so dangerous as he sleeps. His fingers tonight are bent into fists. I watch the folds of the curtains fill and empty with the night wind, like waves, like long blue lungs. From the patterns and the folds, for a moment or two, eyes and mouths appear and then are gone. My mouth is dry, but I left my glass of water in the kitchen. I slip out of bed and look back at him. In the moonlight dark, I say to myself as a desperate prayer, 'Don't let him wake.' He turns on his shoulder. I hear his breath heavy and deep. I move towards the door with my knees bent, my fingers splayed. Although I don't look, I can sense my distortion in the mirror. I know I look ridiculous. That I am ridiculous, but this is what is necessary.

He brings me breakfast in bed. Coffee, and scrambled eggs on toast with grilled tomato and mushrooms.

'Don't ever forget I love you.'

'I love you too,' I say. I might not be lying.

My head is full of fluorescent light, white hot and smoking. Stephen is away with the Schurmanns for the weekend in Sydney, so I am south at Carrickalinga. I can't concentrate enough to read the morning papers so I walk along the beach instead. The scent of damp seaweed rises with the breeze. Above the cliffs, the sky is sinewed with streaks of cirrus, and the dawn moon, half covered by cloud, is the shape of a closed eye. I turn to face the great northern sky. It seems to curve around me, open and grey. I am living my life as if I were trapped inside a pearl.

He was the first to say he loved me. That must mean something. I cannot see a life outside the pattern I have come to know. I want predictability even when it's an illusion, even when it hurts.

The rollers come in and break, and move like broad tongues up the beach to my ankles where they pull the sand from under my feet. I used to think that waves appeared just out from shore where the swell began to rise. But that isn't the truth. Each wave is born far out to sea in a dance of oppositions: the gravity of the water and the pull of the wind. Then they journey until they break open on a shore somewhere. They tear beaches apart and make cliffs fall into the sea long after the storm that made them has gone. Cat's paws. Squall. Spindrift. White horses. Breakers. Each wave carries the memory of the wind. And now they are here as if they've travelled across time. If I could read them, I could read the past. But I don't want to be able to do that, do I?

———

I want a sweet sharpness in my mouth. So after work I walk to the Central Market to buy epicure cheese. I pass a long table of second-hand books for sale. The first title I see is *The Irish in Australia*. The book opens at a photograph of a woman in Ireland in 1899. She is standing in front of a dry-stone wall looking right into the camera and into my eyes. She is dressed in rags. And the rags have holes in them. The caption says her name is McCaffrey and she is a potato picker. She is holding a rough woven basket. The sight of her chills me. The way her arms are bare from her elbows. The way there is so little flesh there. The way there is just bone.

The photograph is called *One Who Stayed*. Was this the fate of my Irish ancestors who didn't leave? Those who had too much hope? Perhaps they didn't know too much hope can kill you. Before I met Stephen I had no hope. But I have hope now. A different kind. Hope he might be the way he was when we first met. Hope I might find the key to stop triggering his rage. Hope such a key exists.

I am becoming invisible. But I must have mass and form for him to hold me. For him to hit me.

I meet a woman called Sister Aceso at her House of Healing therapy centre. The path to her garden is lined with quartz crystals and is scented with rosemary. By her front step stands an unglazed clay pot filled with wormwood. She is *wermod*, a spirit mother named after the Greek goddess of healing. When she comes to the door, she's dressed in a white robe with a wedge-tailed eagle feather on a chain around her neck.

I say to her, 'I have no hope left.'

She says, 'Hope can be borrowed when you don't have any of your own.'

For half an hour I am face down in a hot spa with a snorkel. Through the darkness I hear a voice, 'Leave him or you'll die.'

They call it separation. But you separate the notes from coins in your wallet. You separate the raw meat from the lettuce and cheese in the fridge. What I am about to start is a physical reaction to separate a single atom from itself. There will be a chain reaction. Heat and smoke. Explosions. Fire.

I prepare. I write a note to him:

Stephen. It's over. I want you to take your things and leave the house. I will be away while you pack up. I do not want you to contact me.

Cassandra.

I put the note in the red envelope at work with the old plan. It's under a pile of new files now. I don't look at the old plan. It was a plan that didn't work. Knowing you have to leave is not the same as being able to leave. I don't want to be reminded of that. The flying moth wants to escape the web of the orb spider. But dies there all the same.

I have to leave my house. I know he might destroy some things when he reads my note. I just don't know what they might be. I can't take everything away in one suitcase. He's not even here, yet he's still calling the tune. The *viola d'amore*. I'm the string that's not being played. But I resonate just the same. I need distance. That way he can't still reach me. Not if I go far enough.

Stephen is recording every day this week at the Schurmanns studio, so I can meet Hillary for lunch.

Hillary says, 'Vivienne is an asp. She was born knowing how to pump poison. I think she might be out to get you. If she can convince Neil that curating community arts exhibitions is superfluous, she'll probably be promoted for saving the department money in a recession.'

'Christ, Hillary. Is that what she's doing? I knew she was up to something. Restructuring and redundancies. They are happening everywhere. They could be about to happen to me.'

'The word in the office is that she might be coming after me as well. But whatever happens, darling, we'll survive. My family survived Poland during the war. They survived the Nazis and then the Russians. Whenever I think, "Why haven't I found the love of my life yet? Or had the daughter I want to have? Or, why is work so difficult?" I remember the stories from my family and I kick myself up the arse. It doesn't mean I just accept things. Hell no. I'll fight if I have to.' She leans across the table and says, 'But whatever happens, Cassandra, we will survive this. We will survive Vivienne.'

'Yes,' I say, 'I suppose I could go back to teaching art. I think Professor O'Grady would have me back.'

'A toast then to survival.'

'Yes. To survival.'

We raise our coffee cups together.

I say, 'I need to ask you for something. I might need to stay with you for two weeks.'

'Of course you can, but whatever for?'

'Because I need to.'

'When?'

'I'll tell you when I know.'

How can I still talk with Hillary? How can I speak with any sense or meaning to my manager or to the artists at Semaphore about their exhibition or to the women at Lucia's café as they make my coffee? How can I pay a bill, drive my car, write a speech for an exhibition opening? Or balance a project budget? How can I do all that when I have bruises on my body?

I wait. I used to wait for my strength to come back. I used to wait for redemption. For someone to save me. Now, I wait for opportunity.

He will be in Melbourne for three days at the end of next month. I phone a locksmith. Yes, he will change the locks on the Friday. I will give him the old keys on my way to work. Yes, he will give the new keys to me and me alone. I will meet him at his office after work to collect them.

For six weeks, I have to stay with my plan. Even if he's kind. Even if he makes me laugh. Even if he holds me during the night when I wake from a dark dream crying out Tania's name. Even when he gives me a silver handcrafted bracelet for my birthday inscribed with *éternité*.

I phone the locksmith. To cancel.

The locksmith says, 'Another time, perhaps?'

I say, 'I don't think so.'

'You will call again,' he says.

Stephen phones me five times a day from Melbourne and once every night. I don't know when the call at night might come so I sit in the lounge and drink coffee. I need to be alert or I might miss something he says. I have to remember what he says. Because it's important. He will test me on it later. To see if I have listened to him. He will say, 'Remember what I told you that night when I called you from Melbourne? I told you then ... you just don't hear me, do you?'

He calls just before dawn. He tells me things had better get better when he's back or he'll leave me. He tells me I give more energy to work than I do to him. He tells me I have failed him. The one person he thought he could call *family*.

We sit on the lounge. We watch *Sale of the Century* on television. We answer the questions. I let him win. He strokes my hair.

In 1973, robbers held bank employees captive in Stockholm. When they were released six days later they hugged and kissed their captors. *Stockholm Syndrome*. Traumatic bonding. All you have to do is lose your perspective so you start mistaking the calm between the violence for kindness or love. Just that. It's all about numbers. Six or seven good days a month and there's no escape.

I am learning about him. He never hits me hard enough to hurt his hands. He never hits me on the face. He hits me where no one can see. And he uses things. Whatever is close by. A saucepan. A bread board. A door. I make notes. I don't write them down. I make notes about him in my head. Every day I learn more. This might be useful.

Vivienne leans towards me. Her perfume rises in my face like gas.

She says, 'I was devastated when I heard this morning about the possible downsizing in your section. Your work there is so ... solid.' She pats me on the back. A *there, there* pat you might give to a baby. She glances over my shoulder, 'Excuse me. There's Neil. I need to discuss conference details with him.'

By the door, a circle of managers opens like two black curtains to let her in. Then they close again.

I go to the women's room to wash my hands. The grime of the city is on my fingers as if I'd been brushed with oil.

Hillary phones. She says, 'You were meant to come to Vivienne's birthday. You would have loved the symbolism. She walked around offering everyone a piece of cake while she had an enormous knife behind her back. It was brilliant.'

I say, 'I wasn't feeling well.'

This isn't true. My foundation wouldn't hide the red welt on my cheek from the back of Stephen's hand. He is changing. He's not meant to hurt me where it shows. I thought we had rules.

I think of Artemisia Gentileschi's seventeenth-century painting of *Judith Slaying Holofernes.* The way she holds the sword as she saws through the neck of Holofernes. She does this to save her people from him. She looks businesslike. She is both calm and repelled. I don't know why I think about this painting. Perhaps because there's no anger in her face. Perhaps to kill when you don't want to, you just need purpose. A cause bigger than yourself.

I wait for opportunity. One day one of us will die.

Stephen says he can't stand the way I cook Scotch fillet. That I don't marinate it long enough. He says it has no flavour. He says it tastes like shit.

I say, 'I don't have time to marinate Scotch fillet.'

He comes back from the bedroom with my watch. He grinds it under his heel.

'Now you'll have time,' he says.

The house is thick with fog. There are no exits in fog like that. You can walk the walls with your hands but you won't find them. And in fog that thick you can't see any lines. So you can't see when they're crossed. And you can't remember where they were. If they were there at all.

I am trying to sense my way to safety. Two fists blast out of the fog and into the back of my ribs.

I tell Vivienne I'm sick and can't come in.

'I need you here tomorrow to plan for the training seminar. Is it serious?'

'No, it's not serious,' I say. 'I'll be in tomorrow.'

The weather forecast is hot, but I want something soft on my skin. And long sleeves. I need long sleeves. I wear a cashmere sweater. I tell Hillary I can't meet her for lunch because I need a new watch. I add a lie, 'I lost my old one.' It's easier to lie when it's not an answer to a question. She might have asked what happened to my old one. She might have seen, then. My need to keep away from the truth.

'You never lose anything,' Hillary says. 'Look, I'll come with you. It's been forever since we've caught up. It'll be fun.'

I don't want her to come. I might have to lie, over and over.

Rundle Mall is busy with trade. The noise of the marketplace. Buskers with their violins and guitars. Jugglers. Spruikers. We walk by a man making toy animals out of red and yellow balloons, shapes that look solid but they're filled with nothing but air. I float along the street. Not the float of being in love. The float of not being at all.

'Hey, look,' says Hillary. 'Isn't that gorgeous?' She pulls out a hanger from a sales rack. It's a blue silk shirt. She holds it up to me, 'Your eyes. That's great. I'd kill for those eyes of yours. You've got to try it on.'

I pull the curtain along the rail of the cubicle and undress. Mirrors are all around me, but I don't look. I lift my cashmere sweater over my head, but it catches on my earrings. I forgot to take them off. I hear the curtain open. It is the sound of grazed brass. It is the sound of exposure.

'Jesus Christ!' Hillary says. 'Tell me you haven't got fucking leukaemia.'

I slide down against the mirror to the floor. My jumper still caught in my earrings.

'I don't have leukaemia.'

Hillary says, 'Christ, Cassandra, did Stephen do this to you?'

I do not want to say 'yes' out loud. Shame has colonised every part of my being. So instead, I motion with my hand.

'So where is he now?'

'With the Schurmanns. At rehearsal.'

'When will he be back?'

'Usually it's after midnight.'

'Let me think. We need a plan, honey.' She sits down beside me and loosens the earrings from my sweater. 'Okay,' she says, 'this is what we'll do. We go to your house now. We get what you need. You're staying with me til he's packed up and gone. I've just moved house and even work doesn't have my new address, so he won't know where to find you. And I'm not in the phone book anyway, so you'll be safe at my place.'

I move my hand to my heart. She knows that I am signalling my thankfulness.

What do I take with me to escape a life? The day I left Ippinitchie River in 1977, I was given two gifts. The first was the mantel clock that had marked the passing seconds of my early childhood. Dad said, 'You better have this. It belonged to your mother. It's no use to me just gathering dust around here.' The second was from Aunty Nell. A holy picture of Our Lady with her sad eyes and the earth at her feet. Across the top is Father Michael's handwriting: *Love is proved by suffering*. That's what he used to say in his sermons. Over and over. His face would light up when he talked about pain.

I pack my suitcase with shoes and clothes that may not match, a book of poetry called *Death as Mr Right*, five pairs of socks and my mother's mantel clock.

I tell my doctor I have migraine. She wants to listen to the sound of my breathing. I lift up my shirt so she can put the stethoscope on my back. I hear her gasp. She writes out a medical certificate for me. For two weeks.

My head is filled with fog. That's what the hatchlings of the dragonfly have done. Eaten me away. Excreted fog with the nutrients of me. I leave a note to Stephen on the dining table. Next to it I place a small box. Inside the box is an opal ring and a silver bracelet inscribed with *éternité*.

'That's it. Done,' says Hillary.

I hear the strings and the bass notes of Albinoni's *Adagio in G Minor*. The minors, the chords of the soul, I don't just want to hear them, I need to feel them pulsing through me. I lie on the floor next to the speakers. I play the music where the pain is.

It's over. It's over.

I am in a rocking chair. I rock and hold myself, rock and hold. I am as soft as a baby. I wait for the world to spring out from behind the door, where I had gone with such innocence, and shout, *surprise!*

Sunlight hurts. While Hillary is at work, I close the blinds. I sit in the hallway in the grey light, rocking away. Sometimes, Stephen's face appears to me. I say to it:

> *I wish you pain, silently*
> *like a prayer*
> *for bringing me here*
> *an hour's drive*
> *and every second*
> *further from home*

It has been eight days. The middle weekdays are without texture. Sunday feels like cold silk across my throat, Friday night like fire.

Saturday is like a rasp. But the rest of the week, nothing. Is it really Christmas Day today? It must be, because I have to phone Dad.

He says, 'Thought you'd want to know. Cousin Teddie missed the bend by the railway crossing last night coming home from the pub. His car's all smashed up.'

'Oh god, Dad. Is he alright?'

'He didn't have a snowball's chance in hell getting outta that.'

'That's terrible news.'

'We have to bury him next week. It'll be in the paper. The funeral details. If you think you might come.'

I do not answer. I know he is reading the meaning of my silence.

He says, 'And Betty Crighton's got cancer.'

I remember Mrs Crighton. She was president of everything around Ippinitchie River: the Women's Agricultural Bureau, the Women's Hospital Auxiliary, and the CWA. I remember her standing next to a portrait of the Queen leading the CWA creed:

> *Honour to God*
> *Loyalty to the throne*
> *Service to the country*
> *Through country women, for country women,*
> *by country women*

He says, 'I s'pose that'll be another funeral down the track.'

'I suppose it will, Dad.'

I don't ask him how he is. In case he asks me.

I have no body. Not really. I bathe it, wrap a towel around it, dress it, feed it, but it isn't really here. There are no longings in it. It walks me sleeping to the shops. It's a thing carrying the breath I need to stay alive. I function. I put on a sock, then a shoe, then another shoe. I walk around the kitchen, not knowing until my foot feels strange that there is no sock on my left foot, just the shoe.

Possessions can tell the story of a life. In Hillary's guest room, Mum's mantel clock is silent on the dressing table. Since May 23, 1967, the hands of the clock have said five minutes to five. I don't want to remember why it tells only that time. Or why it was stopped. But even when the hands of a clock are motionless, and the ticking and the bells are silenced, the universe of space and time are still flowing through us. I can never get back the three years emptied by Stephen. More than a thousand days. Blown-egg days. Now I have the empty shells of all those days of my life broken at my feet.

I have checked *The Gig Guide* in the paper. I say it out loud three times until I believe it. City of Searches are playing Saturday night at the Arkaba. This is the time I have waited for. To go back to my house.

Hillary waits by the front door while I go inside. The locksmith has changed the locks. The new keys are stiff and shiny, opening the doors on a life I neither own nor want. I notice first my Matisse. *The Sorrows of the King.* The glass is crushed and fractured. Lines radiate from the centre where slivers have broken through the print, the yellow of the guitar and the white of the two disembodied hands. I know why Stephen did this. The heart of the music is broken. But in the picture there is no music. There never was. The guitar has no strings.

Emptiness can have a shape. In the hallway, it is the shape of a row of saxophones. In the bathroom, it is the shape of his shaver and brush. And in the wardrobe, a prism where his suits and shirts used to hang. My life is full of holes left behind from his extraction. Holes of blackness where the light has been pressed out. The air in the kitchen is hard and cold like water that is frozen. I can see everything I own around me, but it is somehow beyond my touch, as if it were suspended in ice.

There is a note on the dining table: *You won't survive without me.* The opal ring is smashed to pieces as if it had been struck by something heavy or struck many times. I can't tell which. I get the banister brush. Fragments of fluorescence shine in the dust. I remind myself the colours in precious opal are rainbows. Illusions. A matrix of silica crystals. That's all. Tricks of the light.

Hillary says, 'It's not safe here. You'll need to stay with me.'

'Okay,' I say. 'Thank you.'

───────────

A radio talks softly in the corner of Ali's room in Sister Aceso's House of Healing. It reminds me of the gentle purr of nesting rosellas. Ali wears purple and white. Her jeans have ironed creases down the front.

She says, 'I shall hold your hands now and feel what you are made of.'

I offer them, palms up, the language of submission. She sees this at once.

I look at my hands to avoid her eyes.

'Ah, you are made of amethyst. The perfectly clear crystal that is coloured by contaminants. That's what makes it purple.' She laughs. 'We are made perfect by our imperfections, don't you think? Everyone is contaminated in their own way.'

Her face darkens, stern with concentration. 'Your chi is strong in you. You have good blood. Wait!' In one smooth movement, she slides her wheeled chair backwards across the room to the radio and turns up the volume.

'Racing,' says the voice on the radio. 'They're off to a slow start with Dingo Ted in the lead, followed by Keen Magician, Fine Soprano, and Merely Prudent. At the first turn ...'

I can't believe she can just leave me sitting here like this. I say nothing. And as she glances over to me I smile. Why am I doing that?

Ali chants into the radio, 'Come on, come on you old rooster, come on.' At the end of the race, she flips open a little spiral notepad, which has a pencil attached by a gold chain. She begins to write. After a moment, she says, 'All done,' and slides back across the floor to me.

She unfolds a cloth of white silk. Inside, there is a large deck of cards with a blue and white pattern on the back.

'Please choose a card from the tarot deck. Shuffle first and do not spill.'

They are longer than normal playing cards, and awkward to place one above the other.

'Just one card you want?'

'Affirmative.'

From the centre of the deck, I draw a card and put it face down on the table.

'I am not a magician. I cannot read cards I cannot see. Turn it over.'

There is a picture in muted colours of lightning, a tall building, and two people falling.

I ask, 'What does it mean, the people falling? Is it death?'

'They're not dead, are they?'

'No, not yet. But any minute they're going to hit the ground.'

'This is an image that is fixed in time. We cannot say if they are going to hit the ground or not. We can only process what is before us. And what is before us is two people falling. What else is there?'

'Lightning has hit the top of the tower.'

She says, 'And how long is a lightning flash?'

'I did read that once somewhere. A second, a half second. I'm not certain.'

'In this picture lightning strikes the top of this tower for all eternity. It is the bolt out of the blue that lasts forever. It is the end of illusion. You thought you'd be safe up there in your tower. You trusted it. You believed it would protect you. It took you so long to build, so carefully you laid each stone, one idea upon the other, about the world, about yourself, about your work and then wham! The lightning bolt comes out of the blue. Your tower is broken and now you are falling. Your soul wants to grow up. It doesn't want to keep suffering this much. One day it will rebel. Wait!'

She again slides across the floor to the radio.

'And they're racing at Randwick,' says the voice on the radio, 'and first out the gates are Madeleine Rose, No Panic and Salvation Jane ...'

I think how rude she is. Listening to the races when I've paid to see her. I scream, but it's bitten into silent shapes between my teeth. Not a sound comes out of my mouth.

When the race has finished and she has written in her notebook, she looks at me and says, 'You're not living the life you want.'

'How do you know that?'

'You have come here looking. Yes. Searching. People do not seek me when they are fulfilled.'

I nod, beaten by her logic.

'Are you sad about this fact?'

My eyes start to stream. She pulls a tissue from the box on her table and offers it to me.

I sneeze.

'Ah, your tears are coming out.'

'I don't cry,' I say defiantly.

'That is not good. Too much stuck in there. What kind of noises do you make having sex?'

'I don't know,' I say.

'It is good if you put on a tape recorder next time. It is also good if you record your self-pleasuring too. Then you will hear. Noise is good. There is too much silence in you.' She leans towards me from her chair and touches me in the centre of my chest, 'You pay me, yet I listen to the races, twice, and still you make no noise. This is no good. You are too much the shape of other people's wishes.'

I don't have a tape recorder. I close the blind against the semi-darkness of the city and ask the fingers to show me what this body feels like. What it felt like to *him*. This is someone else's body, not mine. How do I find my way back? No, not *back*, I can't go back. How do I find my way *in*?

The skin on the forehead is warm. I feel the indent. It is an old scar I remember above my right eye. The brow is unexpected, the soft fur of a cat. On the neck there is the heartbeat knocking at the door. *Let me in* or *let me out*, I can't be certain. It does not wish to be pressed. I remember the rise and fall of his quickening breath against that skin.

The lips I know are there, but in the dark I cannot tell where they begin. The index finger crosses them in a *shush*. My collarbone is warm pearl. In the line across my heart I feel the rise of my breasts. A pain rises from the centre of me, sharp and loud. It is a needle, a pinpoint of burning. It is the sun centre, the solar plexus of me. I touch it. It is brass and ice.

The insides of the arms are strangely soft. I stroke them, a fabric you would want to hold against your cheek. On my thigh, there's a healed bruise, the shape of a galah's bill, the shape of the end of Stephen's fist.

I close my eyes and try to think of a fantasy that might arouse me. The face of the actor on the poster I saw last week at the cinema. A shining body curved with muscle gleaming by firelight ... I try. How hard do I press? I am a virgin in bed with myself.

You're a fucking cold bitch, Stephen would say. I can still hear it, but his voice grows smaller. There are new sounds now rising out of the air. Slow at first: the breath of a magpie's wings flying overhead. The ache of the she-oak in the north wind. These are the sounds my body whispers to me. In this warm and honeyed dark, I am alone and in halves.

Last night I had a dream. I reached in through my ribcage and pulled out my heart. It was not red and plastic. It was flesh. I tossed it onto the wooden table in the kitchen saying, 'You useless heart,' and with the carving knife I sliced it open. I did this just to see the spool of ash I knew was inside. The dead flame of what the world has made me. Everything I expected to see wasn't there. When I looked inside, I saw galaxies of stars.

My sick leave is over. On my work desk is a rotting bouquet of red roses.

Vivienne says, 'They came last week, but as you were away, and we couldn't contact you, we didn't know what to do with them. But you are here now.'

In her office, she hands me an envelope from Finance.

I am officially redundant. An arts administrator who has failed. And an artist who has no art.

The white envelope with the flowers has a card inside. I know it's from Stephen. Can I be wise and leave it unopened on my desk? It may have words inside that will hurt me. It may have words inside that will make me feel less wretched.

The card says, 'Every note I play, I play for you.'

I take the card and leave the roses on my desk.

I lie on my side in the dark, my hand next to my heart. I can feel it pumping. All that effort just to keep me alive. I cup my hand over it, as if I were holding a butterfly, and I say in a whisper, 'It's all right. You can stop now.'

Doctor Hedmann's consulting room is white: steel and chrome. The sheet on the bed looks like metal. Can a cloth have hard edges? There is a narrow pillow at the end next to the wall, still hollowed by the imprint of the last patient's head.

Doctor Hedmann has a fountain pen in his hands. It has a dark blue barrel with a chrome cap. I notice the pen because he is pushing the lid on and off. It is so exacting it sounds like the ticking of a mantel clock.

'Your secretary phoned me yesterday just as I was leaving work,' I say. 'She didn't mention what it was about. She just said you wanted to see me.'

'Yes.' He stops playing with the pen and sits down behind his desk, which is bare except for a little china elephant with blue jewels for eyes, and a vase of rosebuds I know are plastic. The leaves are serrated. I notice there are no plastic thorns. I don't know why they don't make plastic thorns.

'Your father ... Jack Noble. He's been my patient for the last three months.'

'So that's how you knew my number. He's been coming down to see you, has he?'

'That's right. I gather you haven't seen him for some time.'

'No, I haven't.'

'He wants to be home ... on the farm.'

'I don't understand. He is home, isn't he?'

'No, he's here. At the Repat. We can arrange this week for him to be transported back to the Laura hospital and from there to the farm. And we'll put in place some nursing care, even though he'll be a long way from the city. But he needs someone there. At home with him.'

'Why? What's wrong with him?'

'This must be a shock for you. Your father has pulmonary hypertension. What will happen is he'll either have a heart attack, go into a coma, or the fluid will build up inside his lungs until he drowns. They are the options with pulmonary hypertension. We just don't know which one will play out for him. '

'What's the most likely outcome?'

'A heart attack.'

'Do I call an ambulance?'

'He won't survive it. Sometimes, people try to find miracle cures. They'll fly off to meet some crook in the jungle, because they think there's hope. We want there to be hope. But I am sorry to tell you, with your father there is no hope. What you can expect is he probably won't see Easter.'

Yes, I'm one of them now, the failed generation of women from the bush who couldn't cut it in the city. So when we are called, we rush home broken to nurse our dying fathers. It's all in the timing: our implosion and their dying. I will go because I want my father to need me just once before he dies. I will go because I don't want Stephen to find me. I'm sure one of these is a lie, but I don't know which one.

Will I be travelling back in time as I journey on the road to Beetaloo, to Laura, to Ippinitchie River? What songs of sorrow might the crows of the ancient mountains of the Southern Flinders sing to me?

I shop in the Central Market early for what I cannot do without. Stephen called it the trinity of the table: cheese, bread and wine. Other things I need less often, but that doesn't mean they are less essential. Others still, I can live without altogether. I just don't know what goes where. I buy fresh coffee. Kilimanjaro dark roast. I smile at this. I am a volcano about to erupt. There is symbolism everywhere in our little lives, but I want to know who or what puts it there. That's the real question.

I fill my basket with kalamata olives and herbs. Fresh bunches of thyme and parsley, and garlic bulbs in case Lawson's Emporium at Ippinitchie River doesn't have them. Am I really doing this? Getting ready to go back? I go to the cheese stall for a wedge of gorgonzola and some cheddar from Margaret River, then to the teashop for Assam golden flowers and orange pekoe. I buy big packets. Tea stays fresh for years if you keep it in the dark. I give my order to the young man behind the counter. I ask him for lemon tea from habit, but remember too late, that's for Stephen. I have to remember there is no we, no us, no Stephen and me. There are people behind me pressing into my heels with their trolley. I take the lemon tea anyway.

At the Atrium Café, surrounded by green plastic chairs and tables pierced with umbrellas, I order my final latte. Above me are panels of sea green glass and fairy lights wired into the shape of an eight-pointed star. I watch the sparrows come jumping across the floor to the crumbs of the morning spilling from the tables. These sparrows live and die in the atrium of the market and must think the sky is white glass, and the green café umbrellas are trees. In just one generation, maybe two, memory can be lost and with it, the infinity of the world. What would a sparrow think if it were set free outside? What would it make of raindrops on its wings or the great shining of the city? Do they know about outside? Do they know, but stay here anyway?

I leave the lemon tea on the table with my empty latte glass and hurry out to the safety of the passing crowd, to the scent of roasting cashews and sharp-edged cheeses and the long bleat of the vendors yelling out their bargains. In the plaza a masseur in his white cotton garment yawns as he rolls his knuckles across an old man's shoulders. The woman who sold me the coffee couldn't see the glass separating me from the world. It's not her fault. You can only know it's there when you're trapped on the inside.

———— CHAPTER THREE ————

The Pioneer

I drive north through the frayed edges of the city, past the broken glasshouses and the 1970s homes of cream brick with their stocky fences and unkempt gardens. Beyond, the low-cut stubble in the open paddocks holds the ground against the pull of the end-of-summer northerlies. I am following the eastern coast of Gulf St Vincent and then Spencer Gulf, which stretches to Port Augusta, the remnant sea of the European dream of a great south land with a heart of water. This is the place where dreams turn to salt. The colonists' and mine.

Hope Gap Road. Dark mirages – sometimes a mirror, sometimes a sheet of silver, sometimes serpentine – slip across the road. I am at Lake View. To the north is my first sight of the Southern Flinders, where they rise up from the plain like scar tissue on the body of the earth.

If I could drive at the speed of light, I could escape into a future time where Stephen could never reach me. Can I, at the speed I'm travelling, still find a way to leave him in my past? I pass a dead galah in the middle of the road. One wing is still moving. But I know it's not alive. It is the afternoon south-westerly lifting the headsail of its feathers, the bone of the wing like a broken mast.

I don't want to enter into this ground.

I turn off the highway and head east through Beetaloo. Beyond the line of crops, the hilltops and gullies are darkened by peppermint box and she-oaks. There are many endings here. I am driving through the southernmost reach of the Flinders Ranges, where the quartzite and shale mountains 400 kilometres long divide like a strike of blue lightning, arcing into filaments then disappearing into the air. The great mountain forests end here, as they reach like dark tendrils into the steep gullies and high ridges of sugar gums, acacias, she-oaks and native pine.

The road bends like a river and the shadows of the she-oaks fall across my path. To the east and west, there are stands of blue gums in the right angles of the fences and in the steep gullies where the plough cannot reach. There is a waver on a hill. The one tree left. And there, a final stand of red gums on the river flat. I feel a surge of rage as I look across the paddocks bared of trees and grass. Did we really have to take so much? Where the hill begins to rise, a gutter cuts into the ground, pink and deep. Next to an old truck cabin, two rainwater tanks, crumpled and rusted, lie on their sides like discarded soft drink cans.

Before my people came, the giant sugar gums tilted their sparkling leaves away from the sun. They still slept at night holding their silent breaths until the light of dawn fell across the forest. The quail still laid her eggs in the kangaroo grass by the river. And the cries of the black cockatoo still tore in two the crackling summer sky.

My people came with their axes and their cross-cut saws, their grubbing chains and bullocks. Scarlet. Frosty. Darky. Lucky. They looked for the finest of the trees. With their shining arms and panting saws, they felled them all.

'Whoa back, Scarlet,' my great-grandfather called across the tracks as they carried the forest away.

I remember the photograph of his bullock team in the forest. Behind the bullocks were towering sugar gums, their trunks as wide as roads. I dreamed I could see them beyond the frame of the photograph where their crests were shedding gold.

I said, 'Where are they, Dad?'

'We cut them down, girl, in '38.'

As I drive along this road, I still feel their absence in these paddocks. And the quail. And the black cockatoo. Long ago, I used to look for them on my way to Sarah's Garden, still hoping. Perhaps that shadow in the grass ... is it them? My ancestors crossed the songlines they could not hear.

I play Ella Fitzgerald in the car. All the songs without saxophone. Jazz was never part of my life here. But what was? Does surviving count as a life?

———————

I don't know him. The body is too small. His eyes are closed. His skin is like paper pulled across his cheeks. The details of his face have gone.

'Dad? It's me.'

He opens his eyes. 'Oh, it's you.' He does not say this smiling. He says it with disappointment.

I try to be cheerful. 'How are you?'

'How the hell am I meant to answer that? Couldn't the boys come?'

'Mickey's in America. Brendan's in Sydney.'

He looks at the ceiling, thinking.

'We're ready to take you home,' I say.

'Who's we?' His voice is a rasp.

'The ambulance men and me.'

'Where's the nurse? There's meant to be a nurse.'

'She had an accident, a prang. Swerved to miss a roo and smashed the front end. Sister said she's okay, but she won't get here until tomorrow.'

'What's it now?'

'Sunday.'

'Who've I got till then?'

I shrink until I am a quarter of my size. The years of my adult life melt away as if I'd not lived them, as if I had no experience to offer the present. I feel like I am five years old again. I say this single word:

'Me.'

He grunts and looks back at the ceiling.

I follow the ambulance in my car from the hospital. This is the last journey home. I don't mean home. I mean *back*. Not just for Dad. For me. The tail-lights of the ambulance are red quartz. I watch them as if they are eyes I cannot trust.

I don't know how to do this. 'This' is an infinity of words: how do I change his sheets, give him medication, be in that house again, remember, cook for him, empty his bedpan, control him, be stronger than him, and watch him die? How am I supposed to do these things and not hate him? Not love him?

The dirt road rises from the tyres of my car and hovers and spreads like a jet trail in the air behind me. I drive up the hill slowly, past the old fig tree by the gate, the car rocking as I manoeuvre over the sandstone reef. The same rocky threshold I remember, only a little rounder, a little higher, a little more exposed by the years of seasons. It's early evening and I see the house astride the hill, cool and grey like an unlit lamp. I want to put off going in. I stop the car behind the ambulance. Later I'll park it under the box tree where it will be shaded from tomorrow's sun.

I turn on the outside light so the ambulance men can see. The garden is washed in grey-green light. The single yellow bud of a peace rose gleams in the darkness against the fence. The ambulance men carry him inside. I wait on the verandah until they are ready for me. A wattlebird rises in a loop like cursive. She is a creature of flowers. In winter, she will disappear. Two wagtails flit above the wild oats along the fence line. There is a tuft of cattle hair on the barb of the wire. I cannot see the herd, but I can hear the sad bellow of them carried on the night wind from across the hills.

Behind me the almond trees are darkening. A pair of galahs fly west, home towards the ranges, their cries like a finger rubbed on wet glass. I let their calls ring through me.

The range is a wave, dark and distant, below the stag-heads of the river gums along the Ippinitchie. The old reds are showing their age. The lifeblood no longer rises above the green clouds of them. They cut back. Cut off. The highest branches first, anything to keep the heart of them alive.

At my feet the shadow of the wisteria is a dark web, trembling on the grass. So this is the place I once called home. This absence. Something made me hope I would be welcomed. I don't know what it was.

An ambulance man comes outside to speak to me.

'He's pretty well dosed up for the night. He's a tough man, Jack. Wanting to come home. Is there anything you need to know?'

'Probably not at this stage,' I say. This is not the truth.

'Don't be afraid to hit him with morphine if he's in any pain. And call the hospital if you need to know anything.'

For a hundred years my family has walked along this path to the front of the house. The doorstep is a red gum slab hollowed out by their passing feet. Inside, Dad is already asleep. I turn off the light.

A little wooden cross Aunty Nell gave me for my First Communion hangs on my bedroom door. It was a reminder to bless myself every night before saying an Our Father and a decade of the rosary. Below the cross is the gold doorknob I learned to hate. Every Christmas and Easter Mum handed me a rag soaked in Brasso and said, 'Polish it until you can see your face in it.' When I leaned forward to look, I saw my reflection: my nose, flat and broad as if it had been squashed against my face, and my eyes like cracks, tiny and dark. My mouth was grotesque like the gutter in the high paddock, pink and deep like a cut. I didn't know that light can bend, that surfaces can distort. I thought reflections revealed the truth. Just like now.

I open the door. On the wall by my right elbow is a white Jesus on his white cross with the font for holy water at his feet. There is dust and a dead moth where the water used to be. Jesus was once at the height of my shoulder. Now, he's at my waist. I unpack my bag and put my picture of Tania Pepper on the mantelpiece. It's safe now. No one is here anymore who can take it away from me. I eat chocolate until it tastes like petrol.

I have forgotten what darkness is. Once the light cord snaps, I can only see black. No outlines, no shape. I know my hand is just above my eyes, but I can't see it. Do I exist or do I have to wait for the sun to return to bring me back to life?

I wake early to the songs of magpies, the light of the morning rolling around in their throats. The kitchen is cold with the blinds down. I pull them, and they fly upwards in a rush like startled birds. I walk along the west verandah. The old whitewashed walls are still free of cracks even after a century. The paint on the wooden verandah post is chipped, exposing the dark of the red gum underneath. Is this where I once sat and dreamed about the light, and drew outlines of flowers on the cement with my fingers? Was it here I chased the Father Christmas seeds as they floated white in the wind against the blue blaze of sky until my eyes hurt from the sun? Until I ran out of wishes?

I make espresso coffee. It takes longer to brew on the electric stove than at Tower Court, but then it rushes through with a roar. I think it will wake Dad. It doesn't. I am slow this morning. I look at Dad's electric clock on the wall. To get this far has taken me thirty-five minutes.

'What's keeping you so long?' Stephen would yell at the door.

'Won't be long.'

'Every fucking time, the same fucking thing,' he'd say. Sometimes I'd say it back, but so he couldn't hear, while I washed his dirty dishes trying not to splash my clothes. All the time, I could sense him there, a dark figure against the light of the security door, leaning over his saxophone case, his body arched and taut as a loaded bow.

The clouds are shape-shifting across the mountains, now a thumb print, now a pair of white lungs. I knock quietly on Dad's door, but there's no answer. I go in. He is breathing deeply, his mouth against the pillow. I am relieved. I want time without him. I want to open things.

I begin with the cupboard next to the woodstove in the kitchen. The door is made of plywood and has chrome handles speckled with rust. The inside smells of cornflour and cloves. There are cake tins with dull black edges and no scent left in them, no warm crumbs left in the corners. There are plastic yellow and green mixing bowls with scratched insides, and a biscuit tin painted white with a cut-out picture of a rosebud stuck on the top. There are no tall jars packed with pear or apricot halves and sealed with golden lids labelled *28-1-1966* in blue cursive. The oven door of the woodstove snaps down easily with one pull. Inside it is cold and scented with soot like a chimney in summer. I don't know what I'm looking for, but I feel empty with disappointment. What did I expect? A jam roll baking on a tray, a thick yellow sponge cake and an apple pie being secretly prepared for my homecoming?

In the kitchen cabinet is a set of six bowls with flat edges painted with sprays of blue and pink flowers. On the rim of each bowl is a circle of tiny raised dots like the decoration on a paper napkin. I rub my fingernail over the dots. It sounds like a bell. This is not the sound I remember.

The sitting room is dark and scented with emptiness. The blind is pulled down and the window closed against the heat. The sad eyes of the Immaculate Heart of Mary look across at me from the mantelpiece. In the picture, she is pointing to her heart, which is crowned with yellow roses, and in all directions radiates lines of gold, like light bursting from an exploding star.

Next to her there's a wooden box with a carving of a shamrock on the front. Inside is my mother's rosary. The beads are very dark, almost black. The circle of the rosary is broken. One end still joins a little wooden medallion. On the medallion is a mandala. The ancient symbol of the mystic rose tree, the fruit of eternal life in Irish myth. The rosary is from Ireland. But did it belong to my great-grandmother Sarah? Or even her mother? It looks handmade. From wood. Perhaps it is a splinter from the lost forests of County Clare. I don't remember how it was broken. I think it happened the week Tania disappeared, but I might be mistaken. I put the rosary back in the box.

The air above the china cabinet and against the high ceiling is sour with stillness. What sounds could ever rinse it clean? Here is the place where the echoes of voices are suspended like summer dust, shapeless and dry. A place where time has eroded every human word until only a gesture of sound remains, the creaking of the roof rafters in summer or the breath of the wind whispering in the chimney. I can still feel the sadness leaking from the walls.

In the empty fireplace of my bedroom, I find a tin with a coloured picture of a grey kitten on the lid. Inside, there's a pipi shell with a broken corner, a thimble that smells like paint, some polished stones, and a toy microscope made of orange and blue plastic. The microscope has no glass. Just holes where you pretend you can see something when you can't.

I make Dad's breakfast, stirring hot milk over cornflakes until they lose shape, then add a teaspoon of yogurt and whip it with a dessert spoon until it looks like yellow baby food. I don't know if he wants me to feed him so I put a towel around him to catch the spills, and wait. I knew I might have to see his body. I knew I would have to empty his bedpan and change sheets dirtied with his shit. I knew that. But feeding him. As if I were the parent and he were the child. That would make me the one in control. Dying can have that much power.

He rasps, 'Give me the spoon.'

The nurse has come. She wants me to watch her sponge bathe Dad so I'll know what to do. Most of my father's body I have never seen. Not even his chest.

'Are you the nurse then?' Dad says.

'That's right, Mr Noble. My name is Kristyn.'

'You're a blackfella,' Dad says.

'Dad,' I say embarrassed.

'That's right, Mr Noble.' She is smiling.

'When Old Grandad was a boy, he saw a blackfella camp back up in the hills from the Ippinitchie. They mighta been related to you.'

'I don't think so.'

I watch her work. The precision of her movements.

Dad winks at her.

'Take away twenty years and I wouldn't be lyin' here just doin' nothing.'

I can't stand it. This old thin body with its disease, its dying, talking like that.

'I'm sure you wouldn't, Mr Noble, but then twenty years ago I'd be running around at school.'

The confidence pours out of her as if it were as easy as breathing. I feel my body stiffen with envy.

'So you're from away, then?' he says to her.

'Yeah. I've worked in Melbourne, and the Territory for two years. That was fantastic. I met Fred Hollows up there.'

'Is that someone I should know?'

'He's a famous doctor, Dad.'

'Oh,' Dad grunts. 'Don't know him.'

I watch Kristyn making Dad's bed, turning him gently against the roll of the sheet. She rubs spirits into the pressure points.

'You're doing really well, Mr Noble,' Kristyn says.

'I'm just bloody lying here, nothing clever about that. You're the one shovin' me about. Will the girl have to do this?'

'Yes. Your daughter, *Cassandra*, has offered to do this for you. And every few hours she'll rub you down with spirits so you don't get bedsores. That's why I've asked her to watch today so she'll know exactly what to do.'

He grunts into his pillow.

'What about the climate?' I ask her. 'How did you handle the heat of the tropics?'

'You have no choice. You just have to get used to it.'

'Like dying,' Dad says.

I want to pretend I didn't hear. I don't want him to say that word out loud where it could ricochet off the walls in any direction so I might have to duck or be hit by the force of it.

The sponge in her hand continues to move gently across his shoulder. She looks at him, not with sympathy, but with an expression I cannot name.

'That's right, Mr Noble. Just like dying.'

In the northern sky there is a moon thin and white, like a cat scratch on skin before the blood comes. All day long the galahs in the box tree have partied and panicked in their secret world. They rise into the air, wheeling together in flashes of light and dark like a school of fish. How do they turn like that, so perfectly in unison?

Today, I have seen my father's body, the secret places always hidden from me.

I say to Kristyn, 'Will I really have to do that?'

'The rub down? Absolutely. You can do it,' she says.

'I can tell he doesn't want me to. He always used to say to me, "If I die with my boots on don't cry." And now he can't even turn over in his own bed without help. I remind him of everything he's lost.'

'Without you, he'd be in hospital. He knows that.' Kristyn stands and walks to the end of the miner's couch. 'How are you going in there?'

'I don't know,' I say. I look up at her as she stands next to me. I cannot lie to that face. I say, 'Not good.'

'Can you close your eyes and take some slow easy breaths? And hum as you exhale. It will help.'

'Ok,' I say. I close my eyes, but I don't see darkness. It seems like I am looking at the sun through a thick red blind. My outward breaths are jagged and the sound of my humming is self-conscious and small. It reminds me of someone holding on with all their strength trying not to cry.

'How are you now?' she says.

'I feel like one giant bruise. I didn't know I was in so much pain.' The absurdity of my words makes me start to laugh. The sound is sad and dry. I don't want to think anymore about me and my pain. Even letting it go is still thinking about it. I want to find a place where I can shut it out. I don't know if there is such a place.

I am aware now my head and shoulders are leaning forward. I am losing my balance as if I am about to faint.

'It's okay,' she says. 'I won't let you fall.'

I feel her hand against my forehead holding me up. Taking my weight. I resist. I have to. I have to support myself. I have to not let go.

I suddenly feel desperately sad. Because, apart from Hillary, this is the most kindness anyone has shown me in a long time. What kind of life must I have for it to contain so little love?

I say, 'Being back in this house is confronting. It makes me think about the past.'

'I read in the case notes your mother died a long time ago. You must have been very young.' Her voice has a slow rhythm now. In the vermilion world of my closed eyes, my outward breath slows.

'I was seven. One day, I saw her in the hospital. But I can't remember anything that happened. Then, she just wasn't here. She wasn't anywhere. As if she'd disappeared.' I am loosening and the words slip through, 'Just like Tania.'

'Tania?'

'My best friend when I was at school.'

'She disappeared?'

I am dazed. I'm not used to having anyone ask me questions that burn into the dark shadows of my life. I want the shadows there, then I don't have to see what's in them. So, I deflect the light away with a question. 'How do you do it? Look after the dying knowing they'll never get better. How do you do it and not break?'

'I understand them,' she says, 'I know what dying is.'

I am learning about the pressure points on the body of my father.

But what about the pressure points on his heart and soul? When I was a child, I never knew where they were. They shifted. They changed colour. But they were not like a rainbow or a mirage. They were there. I knew that. Because they could be pressed. By me. Just like Stephen's.

Dad and I do not speak. My hands shake. I rub him with methylated spirits. All the points of the body where the circulation dies from too little motion. I pretend he is not my father. Is he pretending this woman touching him like this is not his daughter? I look at him, this withered body, and remember him at the washstand on the verandah after Mum died. His shirtsleeves rolled up high on his biceps. Frederick McCubbin's second panel of his painting, *The Pioneer*, has the arm of the man in light. The power of him illuminated. Celebrated. This arm felled a forest. I remember the way Dad turned the soap in his hands and rubbed his arms in circles until they were white with lather. I remember the sound; the slap of the soap and his skin together, and he did it with such care and attention, not a drop spilled. He didn't know I was there.

The she-oaks used to grow on ground deemed useless: the stony ridges, the crest of the hill too steep for crops, the sides of the gullies where the overflow of winter rain rushed by. But they grew old, and the sheep drew the young seedlings from the ground, until the last of the wild she-oaks grew only in one place on the farm. The highest point. Sarah's Garden.

I remember when I was seven years old looking up at the she-oaks on the hill thinking they don't have branches. They are an old woman's hair, a young woman's hair, my hair in the wind without the blue ribbon tying it down. Dad must have felt like his body was made of steel and fire when the blade of the chainsaw went in screaming.

'You bloody bitches. This'll shut you up. By Christ it will.'

I remember seeing the smoke from the verandah.

'Where's that coming from?' I asked Brendan.

'Dad's cut down the she-oaks.'

Later that night, I went outside to the gate in the house paddock and watched the tents of red fire. I whispered in the dark to them as they burned. I told them how I'd seen him at the washstand after he'd come back from cutting them down. How he didn't know I was there. Watching him. Hating him.

Kristyn says, 'It's good of you to leave the city to come here and look after your father. A lot of families I see don't do anything for each other.'

I want her to think the best of me. I don't know why. I want her to see me as the caring daughter. But that's not true. It's a long way from being true.

I say, 'I had to get away ... I had to leave my house. It wasn't safe for me there. But I'm alright here. Stephen, my ex, doesn't know about Dad. I told him Dad and I were estranged. That was something he understood. He hadn't spoken to his mother since he ran away from home when he was fifteen. So me being here doesn't make me the caring daughter. It makes me a survivor.'

'Well, whatever happened before is gone. You're here emptying his bedpans every day. Turning him during the night. You're a caring daughter now.'

Dad says, 'There's a letter came for you awhile back. In the tea towel drawer in the kitchen.'

My first thought, *It's from Stephen.* The old adrenalin charges, drumming through my chest. *Does he know I'm here?*

But it's not from Stephen. The handwriting is old-style cursive. The postage stamp is dated 1984. It's seven years old. It's from Aunty Nell.

'Why didn't you post it to me, Dad? They do actually deliver mail from Ippinitchie River to Adelaide.'

'We buried her, you know, not far from your mother,' Dad says.

'I heard,' is all I say. I put the letter unopened on the mantelpiece next to the picture of Tania Pepper.

By early afternoon, the south-westerly has come up from the river, lifting spirals of white dust that twist and billow from the road and then disappear into the flowing air. While Dad is sleeping, I drive into town.

71

The colours of the main street are peeling. The glass shopfronts are pasted with newspapers. Cobb, the butcher, is closed, and the blinds of Fidget's Bakery rolled up, one corner of the torn canvas flapping in the wind. No gumballs now in the red lolly machine, no shiny white refrigerators in the window of Cunningham's Electrical Store. Lawson's Emporium is now called the Ippinitchie Service-Mart. The old wooden counter with the gold measure along the edge has gone. There is a single check-out with silver railings so people can be served faster. The new owners probably don't understand: the local people don't want to be served faster. They shop on a Friday when it's busy, because they know everyone else will be there.

I don't talk to anyone, because I don't want their sympathy about Dad, and I don't want them asking me about my life in Adelaide. I wear sunglasses and a hat so they think I am a stranger from out of town. But I am, aren't I? They don't recognise me. Moira McKenzie is by the stand of canned apricots. Not buying anything. Just there, talking to a woman I don't know. In all the years since I left, the voices haven't changed. Moira is still loud. She says she'd heard the latest about Betty Crighton's cancer from Mrs Hunt only this morning. She announces, 'It's just a matter of time.' As I'm paying for some lip balm for Dad, I hear Moira say, 'And it's the same for poor old Jack Noble. Only worse.'

I walk to my car and pass the visitor guide. Two panels behind glass. I lean forward to see past my own reflection. *The History of Ippinitchie River* says the sign, painted in black cursive copperplate. There are photographs of horse and bullock teams and, to my right, a picture of the enormous body of a sugar gum lying on a log trolley, felled for the Burra copper mines. The loggers are standing over it as if it were a kill. I count the faces in all the photographs. Forty-five.

There is not one woman. I feel the rage roar inside me. They are not here. No mother Clare, no grandmother Mary, no great-aunt Nell, no great-grandmother Sarah. History has buried deep the women of my line.

Outside the Ippinitchie Hall, the young stone soldier stands watch over the names of the fallen from World War I. *A.E. Quinn* and *C.W. Quinn* are carved in black against the marble. Albie and Charlie. Sarah's sons. Aunty Nell's brothers. My great-uncles. Killed at Fromelles in France in 1916.

Aunty Nell said to me once, 'I lost two and a half brothers. Poor Jimmy was never the same. He came back missin' a whole lot more than just his leg. He even lost his name. He's been called Hopper for so long now, a lot of people around here wouldn't even know his real name is Jimmy. But he had no right being over there in the first place. He put up his age just so he could enlist. He said he wasn't lettin' Charlie and Albie go on their own. Sarah said to them before they left, "Whatever you do, don't stay together. If you have a bad one, we could lose you all in one night." Charlie just shook his head, then he laughed and said, "Hell, Mum, you wouldn't miss these two anyway. Albie's never done a day's work in his life. And you'd have a helluva lot more tucker to go round without young Jimmy." Charlie wanted to see the world. The other two just followed like sheep.'

Aunty Nell once showed me a photograph of the day this statue was unveiled, just over a year after the war ended. Along the street were the waiting horses harnessed to their buggies, their heads bowed low. And nearby, the first generation of cars, dark Lizzies, were parked in broken lines. Sarah is somewhere among the crowd. This memorial is the closest thing she will have to a grave for two sons. The people stand together under umbrellas, no faces to camera. Afterwards, Sarah would have driven her buggy home in the rain. Somewhere in a cemetery in France, the destroyed bodies of Charlie and Albie Quinn are tangled in the ruins of a thousand other bodies of other families' brothers and sons and great-uncles.

I look up at the memorial. All those names. The stone soldier will stand guard over them for all eternity. No harm will ever come to them again.

From the farmhouse gate, I can see the sorrow of birds.

Two crested pigeons walk in circles on the verandah calling deeply in their throats. The body of one of their kind is on the cement in front of them, its neck flung back, limp and arched. It must be one of their family. On the kitchen window there is a white smear in the shape of open wings. This bird is dead because it didn't know about the alchemy of glass. It couldn't see the Flinders Ranges and the curve of the paddocks were already in its past. When I hear the air whistle through their wings I know they have gone. I carry the body to the fence of the home paddock and put it on the ground. The bird has green and purple opal on its wing, and the feathers on its breast are grey and fold against each other like stratocumulus cloud. An overcast sky always just above the heart. Ants will do their gathering now. They will enter the body through the eyes, following the path of light to the dark inside.

I go to the tap by the rainwater tank to wash my hands. As I put my hand out to catch the water, a spider, like a big black flower, falls open on my fingers. I shriek and toss it to the ground.

I don't know why I tell him.

'What'ja expect? Rose petals to come outta there? You're not in the city now,' he says.

I don't know what I keep hoping for.

The wind floats in from the ranges scented with leaves and earth, and settles in the box tree by the barn. Kristyn and I are sitting on the west verandah in the light and shadows of the wisteria. A wave of galahs bursts into their glassy songs as they pass us by.

I say to Kristyn, 'Sometimes when I see the ranges like this, with the cloud falling over them, it feels like there's no other side, that they're a wall at the end of the world. And this is all there is.'

'What would be so bad about that?' she says.

'It doesn't feel like I belong here. I don't know where I belong. I felt like an immigrant in the city as if I couldn't understand the language. And everyone I knew was afraid. We were all afraid of losing our jobs, afraid of not knowing the right people, afraid of knowing the right people for too long until suddenly one day, they're the wrong people. Just before Doctor Hedmann told me about Dad, I was made redundant. My manager, Vivienne, said to me the day I left, "Bad luck you couldn't cut it." What was I meant to cut? I think she meant my colleagues' throats. I didn't know how to be that ruthless. And that's what it takes now – to rise in the workplace.' I sound bitter. 'The city is a place of cunning.'

'Everywhere is a place of cunning. When I was doing my training, I worked with a bitch of a sister and she tried to blame me for a mistake she'd made with a patient. It was the wrong medication, but she said I'd administered it. Easy way out. Blame the Abo. For a week, we didn't know if he'd lose his sight. He didn't in the end, but it was so close. She invited me down the pub a few days later and said sorry. She said it was sheer bloody terror that made her blame me. I accepted her apology, then I poured a jug of beer over her head just the same.' Kristyn smiles. 'She took it though. She knew she deserved it.'

'How do you live with betrayal and not be bitter?'

'I don't know,' she says.

It is dusk when they come like a squall. Five thousand galahs. Kristyn and I go outside to watch them. Their moving shadows fill the yard deep as a rain cloud. The light and dark of their wings flash above me, before shearing off the top of the hill and banking across the Ippinitchie in a screaming rain. In the bare branches of the red gums the birds land unsettled and screeching. Their sound is water, not a creek tumbling quietly over the stones, but a flooding storm, the type that makes the waters of the Ippinitchie roar. A storm that, just like death, makes you stop and look in awe.

I want to clean things. I start with what I think is most important. I sweep the kitchen. The sound of the broom bristling on the lino is like a woman panting. She is running. She is seeing the truth in her sleep. The corner by the stove is veiled with web and a cluster of egg sacs like unpolished pearls. I brush them away with the broom. In the sink cupboard, I find an old wire suds-maker with chips of yellow soap in it. I fill the sink and beat the water with the suds-maker. While the water is hot, I wash down the table and the stove. On the windowsill, there is a vase filled with dirty plastic roses. Red, yellow and pink, and a single green fern leaf, the size of my open hand. At the bottom of each plastic flower there are wings and bodies of tiny flies. I suddenly feel very sad when I see them there. I take down the canisters from the mantelpiece above the woodstove. They are in descending size. *Flour, Sugar, Coffee, Tea, Salt.* The staples of life. If only it were so simple. But what we need to keep us alive can be so complex, so changeable. Stephen would be so penitent in my arms. *I'll never hurt you again.* All the canisters are empty except one. *Salt.* It has returned to crystals I cannot break.

The north wind, the bastard wind, howls and moans in the orange trees, and the ridges and gullies of the ranges disappear in a red smear. What is dust? Where are the seeds in it? If I sifted it, would I find them in the sheddings of the earth? The north wind is the sound of loneliness. It is the sound of absence. But soon, it will come. The most miraculous of changes. The brown summer to green grass.

It's the first time in two days I've had to empty Dad's bedpan. His body is slowing down. He doesn't want to eat so I bring him warm tea in a plastic mug with a lid. I hold the back of his head up while he drinks. I am thinking, *Here I am with my losses*. Stephen. My home in Adelaide I can't afford to keep. My work. And he knows nothing about any of it. He hasn't asked, and I haven't offered. I keep secrets from him. It's tempting to do that. Secrets can hide vulnerabilities. And they hide mistakes.

He looks at the photograph of Mum next to his bed and says, 'She worked, your mother. By cripes, she knew what work was.'

She is young in the picture, about twenty. She is wearing white beads around her neck, and her hair is like Katherine Hepburn's.

'Yeah, Dad. I remember.'

'More than a man deserved.' The blue of his eyes is paler than I can remember, without the cruel edges that could make me bleed inside. His eyes fill with water. I wonder if his secrets are full of grief. Not once did I see him cry over Mum. It was just one more reason to hate him.

I ask, 'Was there any warning she was sick?'

'She had some pain in her chest, but she thought it wasn't anything to worry about. So we didn't take any notice.'

'You found her ... when she collapsed?'

'In the kitchen by the stove. She was makin' you an apricot pie.'

'Was she really? Just for me? But it wasn't my birthday or anything.'

I want to cry.

He nods and shuts his eyes. I can read him now. It's his signal he's had enough. I put the mug of tea on the side table by his bed. I wipe his mouth with a tissue and rub some cream in where his lips are cracked.

'You rest now,' I say.

I stroke his forehead until he sleeps.

I go outside. Not to read the sky to see if the sheep should be let loose in the scrub, or if the reaping should go on all night to beat the rain. I don't want to measure this sky. I want to see the enormity of it. Above me cirrocumulus clouds of red and purple stretch north and south to both horizons. The colour of the sky to the west above the ranges reminds me of ultramarine, my mother's favourite colour. Our Lady of Sorrows blue. I remember Professor O'Grady teaching us about the politics of colour. The Renaissance artists painted Our Lady wearing a cloak the colour of a Byzantine empress, the colour of the heavens. The Romans centuries before had believed blue was the colour of barbarism. Now, it is the most loved colour in the world.

Already the limbs of the red gums along the river are changing to black filigree in the leaving of the light. Too soon. Too fast. When there is nothing to hold on to. Five crows fly against the hills. They turn to light in rhythm, flash and then turn black again. Lamps turned on and off. On and off. I think of Dad inside on that bed with his blue eyes in mourning. And now I wonder, in the months after Mum died, did he cut down the she-oaks because he was mad with grief?

I stay up late sitting on the verandah. The shadows of orb spiders crawl down from the trees between the clusters of black leaves. I walk out into the dark. Above me the great river of space and stars shimmers into infinity. I look for the constellations I remember. The Seven Sisters. The Southern Cross. For reassurance the world isn't shifting on its axis. I think how every particle of light is a star burning itself into oblivion. I have stopped wanting him to die.

Dad's room is veiled with moonlight and the breeze is a breathing wave on the curtain, flexing like muscle. Against his bed, Kristyn leans forward from her chair, her hands crossed, her face resting into her right elbow. It is the posture of a child dreaming at school listening to music. In an adult it is the posture of exhaustion. Dad's head is tilted back on the pillow. His mouth is open.

At the threshold of the room, I stop. I don't know why. Perhaps I'm breaking the intimacy of sleep. I realise moments have passed and I have not moved. I am looking at something. No. I am looking at some*one*.

I see first the hands. The silver ring on the middle finger shining like mercury, and the left forearm, the perfect line of it, the dark oak of the skin against the white of the sheet. The gentleness and power there. The arc of the sleeve opens like a mouth into the curve of the triceps. The shoulders. The face I cannot see. I am motionless until a tremor comes. Then my arms cross over my breasts, and my fingers clasp loosely under my throat.

'Oh ... oh,' I say. And suddenly, I remember standing in front of the violet light of Clara Southern's *An Old Bee Farm* in the National Gallery of Victoria feeling the waves, charged and thundering roll out of me, not knowing what to do with all that longing.

I feed my father with a spoon. I have mixed together stewed apple and ice-cream until they're almost liquid. I have a napkin under his chin to catch the drips. When he's had enough, he waves his hand for me to stop. We do not speak. We do not look at each other.

It is late in the space between afternoon and evening where the light is long, a flame golden with dust. On a side table between us are two cups of tea too hot to touch.

Kristyn says, 'You know he doesn't have much longer.'

'What do I do? Do I call you?'

'I'll come, but I can't do as much as you can. Just be there. He probably won't say it, but that's what he needs. He'll let you know if he wants anything more.'

From beyond the gate, the soft grey sounds of the crested pigeons come in on the wind. I watch an orb spider in her web, the tiny claws of her front feet winding her thread over a little parcel of silver. A moth or a fly. Something alive, that wanted to live, met death in her net.

I dreamed last night I saw a cloud a trillion miles long and at its heart was the shape of waves and out of the waves stars were being born. Who should I tell?

My father is purple, the colour of a bruise. He was always afraid of water, and now he's drowning. The river rises in his old lungs scarred by sawdust and tobacco smoke. But I can't throw a lifebuoy that far. And there is no bridge. There is only the river.

There are two lines of stratus now in the western sky, grey-white with reflected sun and dazzling spaces of deep blue where tendril clouds of mares' tails send out their white flares. Soon the rain will come.

I am sitting on the verandah searching for lightning. A wave of grey-black nimbus cloud rolls in across the range, and a green mist sparks at its base. The white and blue of the cumulus clouds disappear into a surging grey. The thunder drums and rolls, cracks and breaks across the southern sky. Single drops the size of a coin break open, the colour of rust on the ground. They shatter on the iron roof. Galahs hurry and cry in the moving air as if they're afraid. They might be looking for a place of shelter. They might be like me.

I go inside to check on Dad. I have left the radio on next to his bed so he can hear the Anzac Day march.

I hold the morphine cup to his lips.

'No good ... no good,' he says.

I wipe his chin.

'It'll hurt too much if you don't take it, Dad.'

'I'm over hurtin'.'

I feel his brow. He's cool. His breathing is rasping, but that's how it's been for two hours now.

'I'll call the ambulance or Kristyn if you like?'

'What'll that do? Save me?'

He pulls at my sleeve.

'Get me outside.'

'Outside? It's just started to rain. What do you want to go outside for?' The panic rises in me, the demands of the father that can never be met.

'Get me outside.'

He raises his head from the pillow.

'I can't, there's no wheelchair. Maybe when Kristyn comes, she'll do something.'

'Get me some water then.'

I go to the kitchen and take a glass from the cabinet and half fill it with rainwater at the sink.

'The best drop in the world,' I call. I am trying to be light, frivolous. I am trying to change his mind. By the time I get back in his room, he is sitting up on the bed. 'What are you doing?'

'Outside. I'm goin' whether you help me or not.'

'Come on, get back into bed. You're not allowed to walk.'

His arm is bone. The skin hangs loose where the muscles that filled me with terror used to be. Even now he can push me away. Even with these withered arms.

'I'll ring Kristyn,' I say.

'Outside,' he says and swings his legs to the floor.

He leans forward suddenly, but his legs give way. I catch him by the waist just centimetres from the floor.

'Dad, please, please get back into bed.'

He sweeps me away with his arm.

'Carry me.'

'I can't. Don't ask me to do this. Please don't.' I try to lift him up from the floor with my back bent, my arms around his waist. I grip him, loosely, afraid of hurting him. Afraid of failing. A sob cracks open in my throat, and closes again. 'I can't. I can't. It's impossible.'

He looks up at me. His eyes set hard like rivets. The look that once so frightened me. The look of his contempt. The look of his disappointment. But I see now, he is not looking at me. He is just looking. Determined. I put my arms around his waist and draw him gently up and as I sit back on the bed, he is on my lap.

'Okay, I'll try,' I say.

'Tryin's for the weak.'

I breathe deeply, then lean forward on the edge of the bed until I feel my feet are ready to take his weight. I place my left arm under his knees, the other around his shoulders. With one swift movement I push forward and rise to my feet. I use the momentum of the rise to step forward ... one ... two ... three towards the bedroom door. I press my back into the doorframe to rest there for a moment.

I breathe in, balancing. 'I reckon three steps to the screen door. Ready?' I say.

'Yep.'

My hands are sweating from the strain. I move my fingers slightly, adjusting. My stomach muscles pull in pain. The screen door opens to my shoulder.

Outside on the verandah we face west towards the ranges and the slow and easy grey rain. On the couch by the wisteria vine, I set him down, unfolding his arms from my shoulders, unfolding the pain.

'You done it,' he says.

'Yep.'

I place a pillow behind his head. His eyes are shut and his mouth is open tight like a small yawn. The rain sings on the iron roof. The water from the downpipe begins to trickle into the tank.

'I have rainwater for you, Dad.'

He turns his head towards me. The gesture so discreet, I wonder if he has actually moved at all or if it's my imagination. I take a bud of cotton wool and dip it into his glass and wipe his tongue, then his lips. He's drying out. The ground of him is losing its rain. That's what death does. Turns us to dust. We are more water than earth. If we have a soul, perhaps it longs not for the air, but for the sea.

'It's got a bit in it, I reckon, Dad ... the rain.'

He doesn't answer. He is sliding into the space of his own, where no one else can follow. His alone, this departure, this separation, this leaving of his life. The ranges are a haze of dust and rain, the gullies and ridges have disappeared as though the hard angles and sharp edges of the earth have been taken away.

A truck pulls up by the front gate. Col McKenzie runs in to the cover of the verandah. Above the hum of rain he says, 'G'day, Cassie. Thought I'd better open the gate to the scrub, let the sheep in there if this storm turns nasty.'

'Yeah, okay. I did see some green in the sky as it came in over the range.'

'An' I thought I'd just say g'day to Jack while I was at it. He all right there? He doesn't look too good.'

'No, Col, I think he's going.'

'Hell, is he? Anything I can do?'

'No, not really.'

'I better leave you to it then.'

'Yeah, okay.'

I hear the truck drive off in the rain.

I take Dad's hand to cup it in my fingers. I think for a moment I feel something. A sensation from him. As if he's holding on. To me? To life?

His face is the colour of white pearl. There is no breath, no sigh. In his throat, his pulse ticks away in a circle the size of a coin. This motion is all that is left of him. Now it is light like the wing of a moth beating. Now, I don't know if it's still there.

The breeze is a south-westerly coming from the Ippinitchie, and I feel it first on my shoulders and then my face as I turn to meet it. I look to the north-east. The end of a rainbow has coloured the box trees with damask and violet where the galahs are rocking upside down, catching the rain in their wings.

There is a break in the rain. I see the black and orange wings of a monarch butterfly as he shelters by me under the verandah until a sudden wind gust sprays water from the roof and he zigzags across the quiet garden. It's not a dance and it's not frivolous. Every change of direction is a sidestep from death so a wagtail can't take him in its bill.

Now it comes rising, the magic of rain on dust, pouring out of the earth in an uprush of scent, clear and sweet. Around the house – the orange and almond trees, the box tree by the barn – it comes, the scent of wet earth, of honey, rising from the light and dark of the ground. For a long time the scent of rain stays. I stand up and breathe it in. I want to hold it in me like the detail of a painting so the memory of it is so strong I can bring it back whenever I need it.

'See you, Dad,' I say. To nowhere.

———————

I have no mother or father now. I am no longer anyone's daughter. This is both a responsibility and a liberation.

I miss my mother all over again. This is what death does. It brings back all the grief, every dark curd of pain that has been hidden away. I thought it was buried deep enough. But it never is. I can remember the colour of my mother's voice. Vermilion. The sharp red of her lipstick. And the motions of her voice. I remember how they were short and close together like the waves in her permed hair. I remember the song she sang on Friday afternoons as she hung her apron in the kitchen, and dressed to go shopping in the town.

On the first day of spring
You shall go to Tobar Bride

Where the mist as white as moonlight
Fills Cill Dara sky.

A basket of sweet flowers
I will keep just for thee
Wild and white mountain flowers
From the meadow by the sea

And your name I'll whisper
each day to the hills and the sea
And when they ask me why the tears, I'll say
'I miss your remembering of me'

I can remember so much about her voice. But I cannot remember the sound.

Already the rain has brought motion. I hear the mole crickets singing at their burrows. By the box tree I find a chrysalis, transparent and amber, as thin as paper. The rain moths have left the earth and taken to the air to breed. I want to take to the past. The women of my line might be in the cupboard in the sitting room. I feel guilt already as I stare at it. Each door has a brass handle, just like my bedroom door, only smaller. I've never touched this cupboard before, but now I want to. Now I can.

The cupboard opens to a scent of silverfish and time. I am an intruder. I pick up a small, green book with white creases on the cover from wear. It's called *Etiquette: A handbook for all occasions to suit Australian conditions*, from 1940. It falls open at a page titled 'Hints for Girls': *Girls will always be teased by their brothers so take it in good part.* I wonder if Mum and Aunty Nell had read this. Is that why they never did anything, because they thought I should take it 'in good part'?

I sit on the floor with a *New Idea* magazine from July 1962. There are no glossy pages with shining colours. It's all black and white like a newspaper. There are advertisements from Barry's Tricopherous for 'sad hard-to-manage hair' and Sabrina Cream for a beautiful bust. It will add up to 3 inches in 30 days. Nothing has changed. Bigger breasts. No wrinkles. Beautiful hair. Lose ugly fat. It's exactly the same. Mum held this, read this. I want it to smell of Vermilion Red lipstick. I want it to smell of *her*. It doesn't.

I pull out a plastic bag with red knitting needles, a ball of wool and *The Schoolgirls' Bumper Book*. In the front of the book, there is blue cursive writing sloped with such precision I think at first it must be printed:

> *Presented to*
> *Clare Fahey*
> *For highest marks obtained*
> *In final examination 1930*

In 1930 she would have been in her last year of primary school. Did she love learning like I did, but have to relinquish her hopes for high school? I never saw her read a book. But that means nothing. I don't paint, but that doesn't mean I don't want to. It just means I don't.

On the front cover of the book is a girl dressed in a brown tunic and a blazer with matching red crests on her pocket and her cloche hat. She's riding a bicycle along a white gravel road edged with oak trees and lawns. The road curves around a gabled mansion with a sharp angled roof and chimney pots. Only the top of the building is visible, because the rest of the grounds are thick with shrubbery. With her left hand she waves a hockey stick. Underneath are the words, *Off to the Match*. There is also a story about Cassandra, the prophet of Troy, and *Wood Engraving as a Hobby*. My mother was an Australian girl in the Depression with barely enough to eat. A girl who walked barefoot to school carrying her shoes so they wouldn't wear out. What did she think when she saw these pictures of a world where you could engrave wood as a hobby, wear school blazers and cycle on white gravel roads? I fumble through the pages. They are thick like cardboard, like the cards of the tarot, but these look only into the past.

Pressed between the pages there's a newspaper cutting with *Mrs Mary Fahey Ippinitchie* written in sea-blue ink. It's an advertisement for the sale of my grandmother's possessions after she died in 1953. So this is what she owned, the necessities of life for my grandmother:

OWENS, JAMES & CO. LIMITED

Have been instructed by Public Trustee as executor of the estate of M.A. FAHEY, deceased, to offer for sale by public auction as above: –

table, kitchen dresser, sideboard, icechest, beds, chairs, chest of drawers, lino safe, dressing tables, mattress, matting, blankets, crockery, kitchen utensils, digging forks, copper, tubs, separator, garden hose, sundry tools, & etc.

A plainsong. I slip the cutting back between the pages of the book. And I wonder how much I really need. Perhaps I need too much.

The flag is lowered to half-mast above the Ippinitchie River Town Hall and the news spreads across the district that Jack Noble has died. The phone rings all day. I hear voices I don't know, with names I can't remember. The morning of his funeral, I pick sprays of gum tree flowers from the grey box by the barn and place them on his coffin, next to the red poppies from the RSL.

Above the noise in the hall, Moira McKenzie says to me, 'A shame the boys couldn't be here. It is a long way, isn't it? For them to come. Mickey's in America, isn't he?'

'Yes,' I say, and sidestep past her, pretending to be in a hurry to attend to something. I am at the midpoint of the hall encircled by people who are all waiting to talk to me. There is no exit.

A man in a police sergeant's uniform reaches out his hand to me.

'Cousin Tom? Is that you?' I ask.

Before he answers, a man about Dad's age touches me on the shoulder and says, 'You don't know me, but I fought beside your father in Malaya.' The man's lips tremble as if he is about to cry. 'He saved my life more than once.'

'Dad never talked about the war ...'

Another man whose chest is lined with medals suddenly slaps him on the back, and says, 'Now come on, Harry old son. I'll get that cup of tea I promised you.'

Bobby Lawson says, 'Almost lost the head gasket getting here, Cassie. I drove over from Port Lincoln this morning.'

'Well, I better book you then,' says Cousin Tom, the police sergeant.

'What the hell for?' Bobby says.

'Breakin' the speed limit.'

'Hell 'n snakes. You wouldn't do that to a fella, would you?' Bobby says.

'I dunno,' says Col McKenzie. 'Last week he booked old Frank.'

'Hell, did he?' Bobby says. 'What for?'

'Not registering a vehicle.'

'But Frank doesn't have a vehicle. He only has his push-bike. Hell, I knew this government were a bunch a bastards, but that's takin' things a bit far ... hey, wait a minute,' he says, grinning. 'They're not the bastards, you lot are. You're havin' a lend.'

'No way, mate,' says Col McKenzie. 'Hey, Frank,' he shouts, 'what'd the sergeant of police here make you cough up to register your bike?'

'Two bloody rounds!' Frank yells back.

Cousin Tom slaps Bobby on the back. 'See, I told you so. When we get to the pub, it'll be your shout, I reckon.'

Bobby leans in towards me and says, 'Apparently nothing has changed around here. They're still a bunch of you-know-whats. Don't ever tell them, Cassie: I may have the shop these days in Port Lincoln, but Ippinitchie and these fellas are always like home to me. Anyway, we can't keep you all to ourselves. The whole town has turned out to say how sorry they are about Jack.'

I shake hands, accept the arms of strangers around my shoulders, and see some old eyes I don't recognise glossed with tears. I thank the CWA for putting on the spread, and Col McKenzie for the eulogy. I do this while I can't get an image out of my mind. At the front of the hall, two old soldiers are sitting by the flowers. They are leaning towards each other as if they were talking about some intimate detail of their lives. But they're not speaking. One of the soldiers with a chest coloured with medals holds a cup and saucer of tea, while the other drinks from it through a straw.

CHAPTER FOUR

The Dance Class

Kristyn and I are walking by the orange trees as the afternoon sun spills across the top of the ranges to the trees along the river. I am still dressed in my black funeral clothes. The ground is soft and my high heels dig in.

'Tell me, Kristyn,' I say.

'What do you want to know?'

'I don't even know your surname.'

'Nurses don't tell people their surnames.' She looks at me with a teasing flash in her eyes, 'So patients can't track us down.'

'Yes, but I'm not your patient. I'm your friend.'

'Touché.'

'I know so little about you.'

'There is something I want to tell you,' she says, 'about why I came to the Ippinitchie, but not today. You have just buried your father.'

'You can tell me. It's all right.'

She leans forward and reaches for a branch of the orange tree. She holds on while she speaks, 'Well, I had a lot of choices. I could've gone back to the Territory. I could've gone anywhere,' Kristyn says.

I'm afraid now of what she might say next. I hear the danger, but I can't see it. And I don't know what it is.

'So why are you here?' I ask.

'I came to find out something,' she says. 'For a long time I didn't want to know, but now I have to know. Without her story, half of me is missing.' Kristyn looks down at the ground. Breathes it in.

'I don't understand.'

She looks up at me.

'I can't finish the story without your help. You told me you knew her, that first day I came here. She was your best friend at school, but then you said she disappeared. I want to find out what happened to her. My name is Kristyn Pepper. Tania Pepper is my sister.'

I feel the world shift. Adjust its stone shoulders. This name, *Tania Pepper*; I haven't heard anyone else say it since I was seven years old. I feel as if I've woken up in a mirage. How can I know what's real if everything disappears as soon as I get close?

Kristyn says, 'She tried working as a nurse for a while, but she couldn't do it. How could she when she was hooked on the deadliest poison there is? She wanted the past to change. That is the deadliest of all addictions. You can never beat that one.' Grief falls over her face. Not like a shadow or an eclipse, but as if the cells of her body have shut down. Turned off their light. She lets me see it and does not turn away. 'Two years ago the addiction won.'

'What are you saying? She's dead? Tania is dead?' I don't want to know there was no adventure for Tania, that her laughter stopped along an ugly road of filth and pain. That's not what I dreamed for her.

Kristyn says, 'I followed her to Melbourne trying to save her. She told me pieces of her childhood. A lot of it didn't make any sense, but she said she'd stayed with a family called the Crightons at Ippinitchie River when she was a kid.'

'So that's why you're here? You knew if you came to this area, one of your patients would be Betty Crighton, Tania's foster mother?'

'No, I didn't know that until after I got here.'

I don't want to see Kristyn's face. I walk over to the verandah post. The white paint is cracked creating dark lines like the craquelure in the work of the Old Masters. Given pressure and time, the fissures of the past will open. Suddenly, anger rises up inside me. 'But you knew Jack Noble would be your patient. And that his daughter who was caring for him would be around the right age to have been at school with Tania. Or maybe Tania told you about me. Did she do that? Did she tell you she had a friend called Cassie?'

'She never wanted to talk about her time here. She mentioned the Crightons once. That's all.'

With my open hand, I strike the verandah post. A flake of white paint falls to the ground. The colours of my pain are the primaries: yellow, blue, and red flowing into one another, mixing until they are an ugly grey.

I say, 'You were so nice to me right from that first day when I told you about Tania disappearing. All those conversations we had. Is that why you've spent so much time with me? Because you thought I might say something inadvertently that would help you? You couldn't ask me straight out because my father was dying. That wouldn't have been ethical. But now he's dead, it's okay?'

'No, that's not true. I wanted to help you through this. Help Jack through it. Anyway, it was no one's business why I came here. It was mine.' I turn around to see her face, to see if I can see betrayal in it, but all I see are eyes weary from too much grief. She says in a lowered voice, 'And no ... that's not why I've spent so much time with you.'

I lean against the verandah post and look out at the sky. I see nothing but grey. Sky and ground and trees are no longer divisible. They are a dark blur. I turn back to face her.

'I'm so sorry, Kristyn, so sorry and so sad about Tania.'

Sometimes, there is only convergence. No matter how unlikely. It feels like our lives are converging like the scattered dust of stars, as if there were an indefatigable gravity pulling them together. Looking down, I see my hand is smeared with the white dust of old paint. 'I didn't mean to get angry. It reminded me for a moment of Stephen.'

'That bloke deserves a jug of beer over his head.'

We look at each other and giggle like schoolchildren. How do we do this? Smile and laugh in the midst of grief? But we do.

Tonight is the very dark of the moon. The late evening rain has cleared the sky. Above me, the Milky Way is a white road to nowhere. The stars are not my companions. They are not lamps that offer the weary traveller hope in the dark. Yes, the light comes floating down on us, but it is dead light. Some of those stars have been gone for millions of years, but they look like they are still out there. Shining. Shining. Shining. As if they were real. I thought Tania was somewhere out in the world. Shining. Her light still reaching me. I look up at the cloud of stars and shout into the light years of space between us, 'Why? What are you all for?'

At the back of a cupboard in a plastic bag is the school photograph from 1966. It must be summer. I am wearing sandals and one of my socks is higher than the other. I forgot to look at them. I was six years old. I didn't know you had to check your socks before a photograph. I didn't know it would look stupid if their tops were not level. I remember Mum saying, 'Why didn't you pull your socks up?'

I have a very bad haircut. My fringe is very high on my forehead. It has a little gap in the middle and a longer tuft above my right eye. All the girls have their arms folded. But I have mine folded so you cannot see my hands. Mickey said my fingers were as ugly as spiders and I'd never find a husband when I was older unless I cut them off and tried to grow new ones.

When I first saw this photograph in 1966, I could not believe the girl in the front row with her stupid socks and stupid hair trying to hide her hands was me. When everyone was watching television, I took the photograph from the table to look at it on my own. There are three rows of children. The girls are in the middle of each row. For balance, the boys are at the end, like bookends, like strainer posts. I stared at the girl in the front row they said was me. It must have been me, because I remembered Mr Henry telling me to take my place beside Agnes Crighton. We were next to each other on chairs of hardback polished wood with slatted seats. They marked your legs with red bars if you stayed too long in the one place. The other girls were different from me. I knew this. Mum said, 'Why can't you be more like Beverly Crighton?' I knew why she said that. Beverly had nothing that needed cutting off. No bad bits that could go rotten and infect the rest of her.

There is a painting by Degas, *The Dance Class*, on the wall above the bookcase in the library. The ballet dancers' costumes are stiff and pointed just like their feet. Ballet master, Jules Perrot, is leaning on his baton. One dancer is scratching her back. Another plays with a red flower in her hair, while another tugs at her earring. The painting says they are untamed and wild without the attention of the master. Degas began the painting in 1873, the same year Heinrich Schliemann found the ruins of Troy. In October that year, the old opera house in the rue Le Peletier in Paris, where the painting is set, burnt down. I didn't know this in 1966.

'Is this the whole school?' Kristyn says as she holds the photograph.

'Yes. One teacher, seven grades. Nineteen of us. One classroom including the library. One of the last of the bush schools.'

'Tania isn't here. Do you know why?'

'No,' I say. 'Perhaps she was sick that day. There's so much I can't remember.' I don't know if this is an excuse or an escape. 'Have you spoken to Betty? She might know something.'

'I'm her nurse. I can't. She doesn't know who I am, and I want to keep it that way.' She puts the photograph down on the table. 'Am I asking too much of you to go back into the past like this?'

'Why do you say that?'

'You are the saddest child in the photograph. Desperately sad. There must have been a reason for that.'

I dream I am looking up at a she-oak. I stretch out my hand to touch it, but it's too far away. But I think how lovely it is. Like a corona light around the moon or the soft grey whir of a skipping rope. The she-oak is suddenly on fire burning bright like red geranium flowers. Inside the flames, the tree has a face. A face with a mouth open in a bellow like a grieving cow. The face on the tree is Tania Pepper's.

CHAPTER FIVE

Obstruction

A coordinate of a life. Not blood or geography, but time.

Jane Sutherland was born the same year as Vincent van Gogh. They both dreamed of being professional artists. And they never gave up. Never stopped. This morning, I woke remembering her painting, *Obstruction, Box Hill.* A little girl is standing in long strips of shimmering grass framed by eucalypts. She has her school case in her right hand and wears a pink dress and a white bonnet. In front of her, a makeshift bridge of four wooden boards crosses a ditch. Beyond, is a rough palings fence and on the other side, a cow (or steer) faces her. Her path is without defined edges in the grass. There may or may not be a gate in the palings fence. Jane Sutherland painted *Obstruction, Box Hill* in Victoria in 1887, the same year that on the other side of the world, Vincent van Gogh was painting a series of self portraits. They were both thirty-four years old.

After I saw *Obstruction* in the Art Gallery of Ballarat, I rushed back to Adelaide and painted *Sarah's Garden.* I wanted to be like Sutherland. An artist who was also a naturalist, who could look deeply into the unfolding stories of the Australian landscape. To feel the touch of its colours. To let in the sounds heard nowhere else on earth. Sutherland trained for fourteen years, and kept painting throughout her life even after she had a stroke. Vincent created 900 paintings. And art historians will forever disagree about what are the most important works of Sutherland and Van Gogh. I know my most important work. And it isn't the one hanging on the wall in the home of Molly and Keith Schurmann.

I place it on the kitchen table.

Kristyn holds the charcoal drawing up to the light.

'It's beautiful,' she says.

'I hid it in the old fireplace in my room until I left home. The chimney had been sealed for a long time, so it was safe there. I knew Aunty Nell would take it away from me if she found it.'

'I don't understand. Why would she want to do that?'

'I don't know. I've never really thought about it. I just knew she would.'

It is night, and as I close my eyes to rest, colours appear in the darkness: saffron and gold, the colours of the ancient sands of the Southern Flinders that have hardened into stone. I don't want them here. I know what they might do. I have been so careful to bury my memories in the dark earth of my body. And now they are beginning to rise, and take the shape of things I don't want to see. Things I don't want to remember.

Every act is the making of history. Not just the ones that are written down. Not just the ones that are part of the stories we tell around the table and the fire. But where do you begin once you decide to look at the past? How can you know where the story starts?

Kristyn says, 'We need to find the truth.'

'Yes,' I say.

I don't know if this is the truth, but this is what my body remembers ...

I am sitting on the kitchen floor on the same baby blue blanket that once enfolded my older brothers, Brendan and Mickey. It has tears in the corners where Mickey chewed when he was teething, and next to my right foot there are little holes made by silverfish in the shape of the stars of the Southern Cross. I look up and see a cloud of burning silver at the bottom of the door. It is late summer and the western sun is low enough to slide into the kitchen over the hollow in the doorstep worn away by the footfall of my ancestors. I want to know what the light is made of. If I can touch it or if it has any scent.

Outside, my bare feet burn on the hot cement of the verandah. At first, this makes me walk faster, but I can't see where I'm going. The sky is red and stings my eyes with grit. I sit, bewildered and hurting, my fingers curled into fists, tight as buds. He comes for me and lifts me up. He is scented with stale sweat and hay chaff, and has arms covered in grey cotton with stains the colour of black tea. His fingers are thick like sausages. His hand slaps me sharply on the leg, 'What the hell are you doin' out here, girl?' He carries me back inside. I am crying now. My hands are curled tightly into the collar of his shirt. *Daddy.*

On Fridays, my mother wants me to watch her dress. So I can grow up knowing what ladies do to ready themselves to win the judgements of the world. She looks at her profile in the mirror. Her roll-ons squeeze a stomach stretched by three babies. *Roll-ons by*

Elasto, a woman's best asset next to her figure. Beneath her stockings, her legs are patterned with little blue spiders of broken veins. Her hands are lined from soap and scrubbing, and are scented with pine polish and floor wax. The endless cleaning of our world. Four rooms, a verandah, a lean-to laundry and bathroom and the long-drop lavatory up the track between the orange trees.

The lavatory is made of corrugated iron with a wooden door that doesn't fit properly and a round wooden hole where you sit. It smells of musk and charcoal because Mum empties buckets of ash from the fireplace down the hole. Mickey says giant red-back spiders live down there in the dark, and one day they'll reach up with their big black fingers and pull me in. He says it's the gateway to hell and that's where God will send me, because my soul is as black as the night sky. He says, 'All girls have souls like that. Just like Eve. Father Michael said so. *Death through Eve. Life through Mary.*' Sometimes if no one's looking I relieve myself behind the barn rather than sit my bare bottom above the hole, and risk both spiders and hell.

Mum leans into the mirror to apply her lipstick. Vermilion Red. She holds it near my nose so I can smell it. She does this because she knows it makes me laugh. It smells like apricots, sharp and sweet at the same time. She rubs her lips together and kisses the corner of a homemade handkerchief Aunty Nell gave her last April for her birthday. She tilts the perfume decanter to each wrist, then sets it back down in its proper place on the doily she embroidered with bonnets and bluebells at CWA last winter. On Monday morning, washing day, she'll whisk it away and replace it with the one decorated with daffodils and horseshoes. She checks her hair with a hand mirror. The double reflection shows a wayward curl from last month's perm at Veronica's Hair Affair. She chastens it with a firm spray of Invisible Net. She likes things to be in their place. Held there if necessary.

I wear a blue pinafore of corduroy with a pink rabbit appliquéd on the bib. Winter is a long way from here so Mum dresses me in white sandals with silver buckles on the side, and white socks with frills of pink lace she's sewn around the tops and a row of rosebuds she'd embroidered down the sides. She likes to add colour to things.

I am sitting on a kitchen chair with my feet so far from the linoleum floor I can swing them if I want, but I don't. I only do that when I'm happy. Today, I want to climb the hay bales by the chook shed and watch the sheep hurry into the house paddock to drink at the trough. I want to see the bore water come out of the pipe as cold as frost. Mum doesn't know why I hate Fridays. But at three years of age, I don't have the words to explain to her why every Friday afternoon I want to stick my head out of the car window and howl, and why the scent of Invisible Net makes my eyes water.

In Lawson's Emporium there is the noise of voices and scattered laughter, and so many colours around me, it hurts. To my left is a stand of wooden cotton reels in navy, royal blue, red, and bone thread. I want the blue one, but I can't reach. Behind me, shelves line the wall with crayon-bright woollen skeins. Young women lean sideways on their hips holding their babies while their other children stand neatly beside them, silent and bored. Older women carry cane baskets they made at CWA with handles covered in red and white plastic cord. Beneath the women's floral dresses are petticoats and coral pink girdles with rows of chrome hooks and eyes. Fastenings. Stays. There are high heels and stockings and above, chafed thighs, where the sweat settles and the skin rubs.

I am touching gold. The measuring tape fixed to the edge of the drapery counter is smooth, like a spoon. The smoothest thing

I have touched so far. And it's like a mirror. In it, I can see my mother's hand is golden. She is next to Betty Crighton and Barb Sanders discussing next week's card night for the primary school.

Barb says, 'There are just not enough bridge tables, Betty.' She lowers her voice, 'And last time the new bank manager and his wife had to wait a whole hour before they had a chance to play, and they weren't the only ones.'

Bobby Lawson calls from behind the counter, 'Mrs Crighton, I do believe you're next.'

'That's all right, Bobby,' Betty Crighton says, 'Judy needs to get home with little Kim. He's running a bit of a temperature. She can go next.' She turns back to my mother and Barb and says, 'I can assure you, there will be extra tables there by next week.'

I paint my lips black with a licorice cigarette. I have chewed one end until it softened. Bobby has a pencil behind his ear and wears a white apron and a green bow tie. I don't like that deep shade of green. I want to paint it with licorice.

Betty Crighton says, 'I see the wool is back.'

Bobby says, 'Came in this morning on the Adelaide train. Dad said I'd committed a mortal sin of business by running out. Half the town wants to knit something for the new babies. He said it was up to me to know Mrs Watson was going to have twins the same week as Mrs Stanley. He said if it ever happened again, he'd leave the shop to my sister.'

'Oh, he wouldn't have meant that, Bobby, surely,' my mother says.

'I think he did, Mrs Noble. Truly, I think he did.'

Betty Crighton says to my mother, 'How's the Piper family getting on? I hear Mrs Piper has come down with pneumonia now, just when she was getting back on her feet after losing Roy. What's it been now? Three years? I can't help but wonder if we need a fundraiser for them.' Together they walk to the fabric bolts leaning against the wall.

A man comes to my counter. His arms are wrapped in wood. He has one leg. It is Uncle Hopper Quinn.

'Anyone 'ere want me money?' He says.

'Be there d'recly, Mr Quinn,' Bobby Lawson says.

I am impressed with Uncle Hopper's face. I have seen it before, but never this close. It is grey-whiskered and stubbled. And he stinks. Not like Dad. Hopper Quinn stinks like the dead fox I found at the back of the haystack. I look at him. He looks back, just inches from my face. He has yellow eyes.

'Hell girl, you're too young to be drinkin'. It'll kill ya. Nothin' certainter. I've travelled the world. It'll kill ya.' His voice is a dry roar like Dad's truck when it's bogged on the river flat. 'Have ya seen me thumb anywhere?' He holds out his hand. 'It's missin'. I've spent all day lookin'. Ain't seen hide nor hair of it. Ya seen it?'

I shake my head.

'Ya ain't? I'll buy ya a round if ya find it.'

I feel his spit as stinking rain on my face.

'Ever been to Fromelles, little girl?' Before I can answer, Betty Crighton is leading Uncle Hopper to the door. There is silence in the shop as the women step back to make room for them to pass. Uncle Hopper yells, 'So you're not going to give me a drink? You're mongrels, bloody mongrels.'

'This isn't the Colonial, Mr Quinn,' Betty says. 'It's next door.'

I don't want him to go. He has bits missing on the outside. Where you can see them.

In the grocery department of Lawson's Emporium, Mum hands her list to Mr Lawson Senior.

He says each item out loud as he gathers them in from the shelves behind him.

'Two tins of powdered milk, three of canned tuna, two of baked beans, one bag of self-raising flour, one packet of tea, one vanilla essence, pudding mix, two pounds of sugar, and three packets of strawberry jelly crystals.'

When Bobby Lawson has carried our cardboard carton of groceries out to the boot of the car, Mum rubs my mouth with her handkerchief to remove the licorice. The skin pulls, but I don't cry. I am too busy to cry. I am looking very carefully at the ground among the pink and brown stones, hoping to find a thumb. I ask my mother where his leg is. She says it was blown to smithereens. I don't ask anything else, but I wonder if smithereens is a place, like Heaven.

The hairbrush is plastic, but it looks like pink glass. Depression glass. The bristles are soft like the hair of a doll. Mum shakes it across the verandah and water droplets blacken the cement. It's an afternoon of shadows in the spring light, not the clear-edged blocks of autumn or the deep grey glow of winter.

'Up here,' she says.

I climb on to my mother's lap.

'Lean forward,' she says.

The brush smells of lemon juice and makes my skin feel like it is turning into pink honey. Aunty Nell is leaning over the peace rose at the edge of the verandah, the kitchen shears open wide and a cane basket tucked into her hip filled with golden flowers. It's the happiest I've been. Later, I smile into the mirror as I watch myself singing into the pink hairbrush:

On the first day of spring
You shall go to Tobar Bride
Where the mist as white as moonlight
Fills Cill Dara sky.

Mickey sees me through the door. 'The girl loves herself,' he says so I can hear.

I drop the hairbrush. 'No, I don't, I don't!' I say, and swear to God I'll die if I ever do.

The kitchen is scented with apples. My mother stands by the stove stirring a saucepan with a wooden spoon. Her arms and forehead shine with sweat. She reaches up to the mantelpiece above the woodstove for a canister. It is aluminium silver with *Sugar* written on it. She is singing *Tobar Bride*.

'What's *Tobar Bride*?' I ask.

'I don't know. They're just words.'

'What are mountain flowers?'

'I don't know. It's just a song. My mum used to sing it to me when I was little.'

'Why?'

'Because it helped make the milking and the washing and the ironing easier I suppose.'

She serves the apples as sweets with homemade ice-cream, custard and a dollop of scalded cream which melts into little white rivers through the custard. The bowls are small with scalloped edges. I like these bowls. They have little raised dots like braille on the edges, and I can run my finger along them to make a ringing sound. I notice tonight for the first time that Mum always serves us in the same order. Dad first, then Brendan, Mickey, herself. Then me.

It's a secret. I am crawling through a grass tunnel to the hideaway by the river, trying not to sneeze. I want to be like Uncle Martin in *My Favourite Martian*. When he wants to disappear, he concentrates, and antennae rise out of his head. I frown and think hard. I want to prowl like the ghosts of the curlew and the quail, invisible as the wind.

The hollow of the red gum is black with charcoal, burnt out in a fire no one remembers. On the right side is a hole, the shape of a diamond, just low enough to see through if I stand on my toes. An invisible breeze puffs the heads of the wild barley. They tremble, so very close to seeding.

I can hear the rosellas feeding although I can't see them, but they're up there in a hollow where a branch used to be. If you didn't know better you could mistake it for a shadow. From my hideout in the red gum I listen. There are bees crawling over the white flowers on a Christmas bush, just inches from my face. Above my right eye, I feel the sting go in.

Brendan and Mickey hold me down on the kitchen table while Dad digs out the sting with the corner of a razor blade.

Mickey says, 'Bees are born stupid. They can only sting once.'

The light blurs from the run-off. I bite my tongue that tastes of tears, but I do not cry. I know somewhere in the grass by the Christmas bushes the bee is already in agony, dying, half its backside gone. And I can't move, even if I wanted.

Dad licks the gravy from his knife. 'By cripes, we're going to have some fruit cases this year,' he says. 'Those trees down by the river flat have so many Christmas apples they're damned near touching the ground.' Crumbs of potato fall on to his chin and then the tablecloth. 'There's a couple of hundred half cases of Irish peach apples down there as well. I want you boys down there after school every night next week with your guns keeping the birds off of them. Brendan can use the twenty-two and you, boy,' he says looking at Mickey, 'you take the slug gun.'

Mickey's smile lights the kitchen.

'But keep together,' Dad says. 'I don't want you blowin' each other's heads off.'

Brendan says, 'Come on Dad, even if he tried Mickey couldn't hit a bull in the bum with a handful of wheat.'

Mum is stirring custard on the stove, 'Must we have that standard of talk at the tea table? You were only at Mass this morning.'

'Aw, at least I'm not like the girl,' says Mickey. 'She's been down there every night this week standin' guard over a nest of them.'

Dad drops his cutlery onto his plate and pushes it away from him. 'A nest of what?'

I look at Mickey. I don't know how he knows. He looks at me and sees that I'm begging him not to tell. He grins.

'A nest of rosellas!' he says.

Dad slams his open hand on the table. 'Hell girl, whatcha doin' wastin' your time on damned rosellas for? Why can't you do somethin' useful like helpin' your mother aroun' the place?'

I lower my head. They will not see. I will not let them see. The mashed potato is so hot it burns the end of my tongue. It's like boiling tea in my throat and it hurts all the way down.

I tilt my head against the sun and the pale grass. White congestus clouds tower above in a high blue sky, the same blue I found this morning on the wings of a dead kookaburra by the gate to the home paddock.

The rosellas won't die. Jesus will save them.

I close my eyes loosely, so the world blurs and the colours of the sunlight can break open on my lashes. Sunshine is a code, just like the semaphore in Brendan's *Boy's Own Annual*. I practised with two of Dad's hankies I'd borrowed from the ironing basket, but no one signalled back.

The colours flash across my eyes. Yellow, blue and red. Father Michael says Jesus is the Son of God. Doesn't he mean *sun*?

Jesus is made of rainbows, the same colours as rosellas. He will save them.

I blink against the light. My eyes fill with water.

Last winter Dad walked through a rainbow. He was climbing the hill looking for Soursob's calf. From the verandah I saw him turn red and golden. Mum said he'd be just the same when he got back. *How can he be the same? He was in a rainbow.* It was two days before I stopped staring at him, looking for changes.

It is mid afternoon and a warm breeze wanders from the Ippinitchie to the house. It carries the sound of sheep, the lame *aaah* of an old crow and the scent of dust and pine. I'm sitting on the mat in the kitchen with my back against the wall reading *Black Beauty*. On a wooden chopping board at the end of the kitchen table a green enamel dish steams with freshly stewed apples. Mum rolls out pastry on a plastic sheet. It has pastry recipes written on it in red lettering. Recipes I don't want to read or learn.

'You should be watching this so you'll know how to make an apple pie when you have a family of your own.' Mum is sharp like green fruit.

I don't look up from my book. On a gravel road, Black Beauty is racing with the drunken Reuben on his back. I can see in my mind

Black Beauty's flanks shining, wet with sweat. Blood drips from the wounds of the whip and spurs.

Mum presses down on the rolling pin so hard she grunts. 'One day you'll miss not watching to see how it's done, when you've got a kitchen of your own.'

I don't want a kitchen. I want to read. I can do that. Aunty Nell taught me. Beauty's mouth foams an awful pink. The bit draws hard and cold. The gravel road sets his hoof on fire. I can see the terror in his face.

'Dad says it's time you started to earn your keep around here. You'll have to start pulling your weight sooner or later. He says you need to start learning about running a house or you'll be no use to anyone. Beverly Crighton helps her mother. Mrs Crighton told me the other day at CWA that Beverly is a beautiful embroiderer, and she can whip up a batch of scones in no time.'

I see him run, bruised, wounded. I look at the picture of him on the front cover and study the long black mane, the proud arc of his neck, and those sad eyes like Aunty Nell's.

'And there's Mrs Cunningham's daughter, Megan. She won the Junior Cake Section at last month's Bureau. She made a lovely sponge cake and decorated it herself with jelly beans and whipped cream. You wouldn't know the first thing about getting a meal together.'

When Black Beauty stumbles at full pace and crashes to the gravel on his knees, I slam the book shut. Not because I cannot read on, but because the wind from the river is carrying the sound of rifle fire into the kitchen. I stand on the verandah listening. Six shots echo against the shoulder of the hillside.

'It's coming from the river,' Mum says. 'That'll be Teddie trying to save his almonds.'

I close my eyes and see the rosellas falling, and hear the soft thud they make as one by one their bodies hit the ground.

At evening, when I offer some mutton scraps to Tiges on the verandah, he meows and purrs, nudges his head into my hand, and glides under my fingers in a blurred arc of striped fur.

'Hell girl,' Dad says, 'can't you see that cat's as full as a goog? I bet he's been over with Teddie cleaning up birds. Now outta me road. There's a stew on the table with me name on it.'

I'm watching blowflies by the kitchen window. They tap at the glass trying to find a way to escape until their wings give up, then with a long hum they slide down the glass to join the bodies below. For a while, they crawl there, stumbling over the corpses until they die. I can't understand why they can't work it out. All they have to do is fly away from the window, and then they would see the light around the wire door. It would be so easy to get away. The door has many holes.

I ask Dad. 'Because they can't learn from what happens to them. That's what makes us different from the rest of creation, although some of us are more like the flies. We just keep bangin' our heads into the glass hopin' for a bloody miracle.'

I want Brendan's *Grade Five School Reader* to learn more words, so I'm cleaning his school shoes with a brush and black polish from a tin that smells like petrol. Over the steam of the sink, my mother hums. The outside light shines on the verandah. A cloud of black flying ants twists around the light globe. They crawl in under the screen door, their wings beating against the table. Some drop to the floor. Mickey is doing his homework for Sister Catherine, colouring in a picture of Jesus ascending to heaven. Every now and then he stabs a flying ant with his pencil. I know that in the morning Mum will take the dustpan and broom from the hook by the laundry door and sweep up thousands of bodies from the table, the windowsill and the floor. But I'm wondering if the madness around the light is because the insects know they'll be dead by dawn.

I am in the kitchen colouring in a picture in my prayer book of Jesus with a child on his lap. But I don't have a yellow pencil for his halo.

I ask Mum, 'Is it all right to use a green one?'

Mum says, 'It's *making do*. When you don't have what you need, you just have to turn to something else instead. Our Lord isn't going to mind a bit if you give him a green halo.'

Dad looks out the kitchen window and says, 'Well, there's the McKenzies heading home from church.'

I can hear their car roaring down the road.

Mum says, 'They're a bit late, aren't they? It's nearly midday.'

Dad says, 'They probably dropped off some tomatoes to Fidgets. Col was telling me at Friday's market he's got a good crop this year.'

Brendan says, 'Look at that, Dad. There's another car behind them. It's green. Looks like one of those new Holdens.'

Dad says, 'Now who in the hell could that be?'

We all rush outside to look.

Dad shakes his head, 'Hell and snakes, I don't know what this world is coming to. It's the second time this week I've seen a vehicle I don't know on our road.'

In the kitchen, Dad turns up the wireless for the midday news:

Police are continuing their search for the three Beaumont children who were last seen at Glenelg Beach on January 26 ...

Mum looks at us and says, 'Father Michael has asked us all to pray to Our Lady to bring them home.'

Dad says, 'Now you three kids, when you're out on the road and you see a vehicle coming, hide behind a bush. It might be a stranger. You don't want to end up like the Beaumont children.'

I ask, 'Where are they, Dad?'

Dad says, 'No one knows. They've disappeared.'

Mum and I are on our hands and knees waxing the floors with rags.

'How much longer?' I say.

She looks over at me and says, 'Remember what Father said at Mass: *Your suffering is nothing compared to that of Our Lord. Wear the thorn in your heart with joy. You must hate yourself and love only God.*'

She crawls across the floor, her arms moving in circles against the green and white linoleum.

> *Hail, Mary, full of grace, the Lord is with thee.*
> *Blessed art thou among women, and blessed is the fruit*
> *of thy womb, Jesus.*
> *Holy Mary, Mother of God, pray for us sinners,*
> *now and at the hour of our death. Amen.*

Her sweat falls on the floor. She mixes it in with the wax.

In the outside laundry, she changes her pad and puts it in a bucket to soak. A spider drops from the ceiling on to my shoulder like a lump of soft coal. Out of the corner of my eye I see its blackness against my skin. I cry out as her hand knocks it to the floor. She crushes it with her shoe. I look, but there are no puncture marks burning red. Dad always says they're too dopey to bite you in weather as hot as this. For the rest of the morning, every crawling drop of sweat on my skin is a spider creeping.

Aunty Nell is here to babysit for the Ippinitchie Annual Tennis Club Dinner Dance. She sits on my bed knitting blue jumpers for Mrs Stanley's twins, while I read *Black Beauty* out loud to her.

'That's a very sad tale,' Aunty Nell says. 'What in heaven's name made me give you such a sad tale?'

I slip down under my sheet. It is old cotton, worn smooth like a river stone. I want to hear a story about Sarah. No, more than that, I want a story that will get me away from here. Here is where rosellas fall dead to the ground with bullet holes in them.

'Tell me about the water,' I say.

'I must have told you that one a hundred times or more.'

'Please.'

Aunty Nell is backlit by my bedroom light. I am looking at her white hair thinking of the haloes in my holy pictures. She puts her knitting on the dressing table and folds the sheet neatly under my chin. Waves of delight curl my body.

'Well, donkeys' years ago,' Aunty Nell says, 'long before you were born, when we were living up on the hill in Sarah's Garden, when Teddie's dad was still alive ... have I ever told you why it was called Sarah's Garden?' I shake my head. This is a lie. But lying is allowed in stories, isn't it?

'Because my mother, Sarah, that's your great-grandmother, she built that place with her own hands, that's why. Your dad's uncle, Uncle Blue, he gave her a bit of a hand with the roof, but by all accounts she did the rest on her own. Two rooms. A kitchen with a fireplace and a bedroom. I still say that fireplace was the best I've ever seen. The only one I know of built by the person who was going to use it. There was a special mark she carved into the keystone in the chimney. I don't know what it means.'

This is the first time she has told me this. 'What'd it look like?'

'Like nothing I've seen in my time. I had a good look at it on more than one occasion, and I remember it had four spokes shaped a bit like sheaves and they met in a square in the middle.'

'Can I see it?'

'Oh honey, it probably got all broken up when your Dad knocked the place down.'

I bite my lip with disappointment.

'Anyway, just like me to get us sidetracked. I was telling you the story about the water, wasn't I? Now there I was one September day 'round about midmorning making spinster's buttons for afternoon tea. I only had one egg on account of the fowls not laying, and I called out to Teddie to come inside. That spring he was three years old and sometimes I'd let him play on the verandah. I could keep an eye on him through the kitchen window. Well, there I was, sleeves rolled up to the elbows beating the living daylights out of these spinster's buttons when I heard a scream that would wake the dead. I dropped the bowl and hurried over to the screen door, but it wouldn't open. As hard as I pushed, that screen door wouldn't budge. I could see Teddie by the underground tank crying and pointing in my direction and as my wits came back, I looked down to where he was pointing by the door and—'

I squeeze the top of my sheet. I hold on. I am afraid this time Aunty Nell might change the story, the way Dad and Mickey change themselves. Without warning.

'Well, I couldn't believe it. Two big brown snakes were warming themselves right there on the verandah by the door. If I'd gone barging out there, the two of them would've got me. And no phone to ring for doctor in those days. I would've been a goner.'

I let go. The story is the same.

'Something told me what to do. Not a voice or anything, but

something nevertheless. Cool as a cucumber, I filled the baby's bath with cold water – the old bath, the one I do my apricot preserves in – and I sneaked back out to the door, opened it with my foot and let them have it. The water all over them. They were off before they knew what hit them.

'I don't know to this day how they didn't hear me coming, me knees were making such a racket knocking together, and the screen door, for the first time in living memory never made a sound. But you know the funniest thing of all?'

I nod. This is the part of the story I love the most.

'When I went to the door the second time, when I had the cold water with me, I'd forgotten all about it, but that screen door opened with me hardly having to touch it. And yet when Teddie'd been making all that din, and I would have stepped on those snakes, that blessed door wouldn't open for love nor money.

'I reckon Sarah was looking out for me that day. I bet if I had the kind of eyes they say some people have, I would have seen her large as life on the other side of that door hanging on to the handle for all it was worth.'

I want to touch her. My right hand starts to move out from under the sheet, but Mum's voice is in my head, 'Don't do that. It's rude. Only rude little girls touch people.' I stop and pull my hand back. In.

I ask, 'What did you do then?'

'I did what anyone else would do. I went outside that evening and looked up at the stars and said, *Thank you* like I'd never said it in my life before. *Thank you*. So just you remember, sometimes things go on that we know nothing about. But they go on all the same. I reckon she's up there on the hill among the stones and the wind, looking out for us, even now.'

Thoughts have a taste. I am thinking about dead birds. The darkness in my room is sour with their scent. I want Sarah to be here. I want her to reach through time and save the rosellas. No, more than that. I want her to reach through time save me. Will she do that?

When I hear Aunty Nell go outside to empty the teapot, I sneak to the kitchen, reach into the fridge and stick my finger into a bowl of icing sugar. I fill my handkerchief with the soft whiteness and go back to bed. By my door, Jesus glows green on his cross. He reminds me I am wicked. I know I will spend a long time in purgatory being thrown about in the sea of flames. And God will be watching and he will be as angry as Dad. I put a scoop of icing sugar into my mouth. The sourness slips away into the dark.

I see Brendan and Mickey hiding behind the rock looking up along their guns to the apple trees. With the first shot, a hundred rosellas jump from the branches together, filling the treetops with wild bursts of red and orange screams. Their wings stretch outwards, the long vaned feathers snap open at the tips in a panic to hold air, fighting for uplift, straining the muscles to push the feathers into an upstroke. The wingtips tilt. The tendons tighten in the rush ... up ... up ... they rise, the air crackling with screeches. Their underwing feathers smash blue and black against the air and the sound of the guns.

A slug explodes through a young one's eye. It is dead before the body is jerked backwards into the fall. Its neck snaps as it hits the ground in a smear of blood and broken feathers. Tiges runs from the rock where he has been waiting with the boys, and grips the mantle of the dead bird with a growl. He lifts his head and proudly drags it away.

'Get a squeaker, get a squeaker,' says Brendan, as he reloads.

A female in the down-stroke of her wings is by the red gum when Mickey fires, bursting open the muscles of her left shoulder. The tendons in her wing release and the sudden rush of air through her feathers throws her backwards into a stall. She screams with terror, and dips forwards into a dive, her right wing in a clumsy push against the air to slow her fall.

Mickey's face is gleaming, 'Got one,' he says.

The flock rises back over the trees in whirls of colour and noise until they are out of range on the other side of the river.

'We'll see if she's any good,' Brendan says. His eyes are shining, but his voice is measured and slow.

I can see where the bird has fallen, a stone's throw from my hiding place. The bird struggles to regain her footing and walks in mad little circles through the clumps of grass. The bird's head bobs forward until her left wing, dragging against the ground, knocks a stem of Salvation Jane. I can't tell if it is pain or the loss of balance that sends the bird tumbling forward.

'Go and swat her. Make her squawk,' Brendan says.

'What with?' Mickey says.

'That branch over there.'

Brendan points to a small eucalyptus branch the length of Mickey's arm at the base of red gum. It is finger thick with a spray of dried leaves at the end.

Mickey strides over to the bird and strikes her with the branch. She falls to the ground on her right side, then rolls herself upwards to her feet, and for the first time since the bullet struck her, she screeches.

'Hit her again,' Brendan yells.

I watch from my hiding place as the cries of the wounded bird strike the sky and the hot silence of the river flat like crimson lightning. The cries are answered. Three birds from the flock cross back from the river and land in the red gum above her.

'Dad said it'd work,' Brendan smiles, as he takes aim at the one in the middle.

The horizon is blurred with colour, white, dark blue and pale grey, the grey of wet sand or a river stone. By the time I reach the Ippinitchie the apple trees are aflame with birds. I sneak through the grass tunnel to my hideaway in the red gum and listen. A money spider spins silver over the charcoal above my head. I am not frightened of spiders today. I am listening and watching through the peephole shaped like a diamond at the shadow where the dead limb forks. Then I see them. Him first. He lands on an outer branch and then with low-pitched whistles calls his mate. Her red head rises from the shadow where the nest is hidden. She moves along the branch to the cover of the red and green of new summer leaves. He meets her there for her evening feed.

I can hear Brendan and Mickey talking, coming towards her, taking their place behind the ridge. I can hear them loading their guns. I run to the river and snatch a handful of river stones, and tear through the grass towards the apple trees yelling, 'Shoo, shoo.' I throw the rocks into the trees and clap my hands. 'Shoo.' My hands burn. The birds rise in a cloud of red and cobalt blue.

'I'll go and tell Dad,' Mickey says.

Dad asks me what books I've been reading because there's nowhere else I could have got an idea in my head to do something like that. And when I say *Black Beauty,* he says to hand it over, and I can't have it back until I've come to my senses, and if I ever do anything like that again he'll take his belt to me.

The afternoon is stale with heat. A breeze lifts the dust from the road as Mum stands by the clothesline untying sheets that have been twisted by the northerlies into furled sails. She props the line against the wind. I am in the cool of the south verandah hearing the whistles and chatter of the silvereyes in the sultana vine. Every now and then I see a flash of luminous green wings between the leaves. Dad has bought a brand new transistor radio in port wine plastic, so Mickey has the old yellow wireless to play with. It has rounded sides like wool bales and is scented like furniture polish. I know Mickey's work is important. He is learning to take things apart.

I am playing the knucklebones game Mum taught me. *Bellies, backs, esses and flats.* My favourite side of the knucklebone is the belly. It is the shape of Uncle Hopper's tummy. I practise throwing my five knucklebones into the air and catching as many as I can on the back of my hand. I miss over and over. But I want to get better at it because one day someone might play the game with me. It is quiet now apart from the sound of Mickey's tools undoing things in the heart of the wireless. Sometimes silence is more than the absence of sound. Sometimes it is the absence of love. I can't help but speak.

'One day I'm gonna plant she-oaks all over the farm so all the black cockatoos'll come back. Dad says they were all over the place once.'

Mickey leans over the screwdriver. He presses so hard he grimaces.

'They don't want she-oaks. They want fruit trees covered in our apples.' He doesn't look at me. I know why. He doesn't have to look at me to see inside me. 'Hell, don't you know anything? That's why they had to shoot them out in the first place.'

'No, they didn't. Dad said they just went away.'

Mickey smiles.

'He just said that so you wouldn't cry.'

'I don't cry.'

There are no tears, just the sensation of a terrible separateness ringing through me. I am alone. It is the sound of a single knuckle-bone hitting concrete.

Mickey says, 'One day when Dad's old I'm gonna clean up all the rosellas and galahs, just like Grandad got rid of the black cockatoos. I'll wipe them out. Every last one. No more screeching and squawking like a bunch of women.'

'No you won't. I won't let you kill them.'

'I'll do whatever I want. The farm won't belong to you. It'll belong to me and Brendan.'

'No it won't.'

Mickey looks up from his screwdriver, with the look only his eyes have.

'Go on then, ask Dad.'

'What about me?'

'You get Mum's stuff. Girls' stuff. Dresses and beads and stuff. You get that. Girls don't get given farms. Only boys get farms. And you're a girl. To get a farm you have to be a boy.'

Tiges mews around my ankles. He follows me into the bole of the red gum, rubbing his flanks against me until he crackles. Brendan is behind me, the rifle over his shoulder.

'They're still here, I can hear them feeding,' I say.

'See?' Brendan says, 'I told you I wouldna shot them. I only want the ones doin' the damage.' I am in the shadow of the burnt-out tree. His head is haloed in the heavy light, specked with dust. 'Dad wants me to get rid of some of the galahs. He says they'll make a mess of the wheat. Come on then, we gotta do this.'

I follow him to the rock. He slides open the cardboard drawer of a packet of bullets and tilts the gun forward.

'This is how you do it. You pull it back like this,' the gun clicks, 'and put the bullet in here ... like this, that's called the firing chamber ... then push it back towards you and that locks it in.'

I am not watching. The ground we're kneeling on is sprayed with little cylinders of gold. I pick one up. There is a grey scar on the closed end where the bolt has hit. It is a small mouth, the shape of a smile. I put it down carefully as if it still has power, like a spider pretending it's dead.

Brendan wounds a galah.

'Go on girl, get it. Make it squeak. '

I pick up a fallen branch. The injured bird struggles to his feet, watching me. In a burst of pink, he tries to lift his wings, but falls.

Three times Jesus fell with the cross. He was in agony.

The bird screeches. It is lightning guilt through my body.

'Shush,' I plead, 'shush. Don't cry.'

Brendan yells, 'Hold the stick the other way 'round. Thick end first!'

The bird says, 'Save me.'

'I can't. I have to be big. Dad said.'

'Save me ... please,' the bird says.

'I don't know how.'

'Come on!' Brendan calls. 'Come on, hit it.'

I hold my breath to be invisible like the wind. My first blow is clumsy and flicks the top of its back. The bird rises, its wing dragging on the ground. A grey mantle, torn and dirtied in the grass. The eyelids of the bird close for a moment. They are crinkled like an elbow and coloured like Mum's pearls.

'I'm sorry,' I say.

When the eyes of the bird open again, the look they give me hurts even more than a razor blade cutting out a bee sting.

'You will go to hell. You are wicked,' says the bird.

'No,' my voice pitches high in my throat where it burns.

'God hates you now, and will send you to hell.'

'I don't know what to do.'

'Save me.'

Suddenly, the bird is not a bird, but a piece of wood, coloured wood, grey and red, the colour of blood and cloud. I raise the bough above my head. I am Aunty Nell chopping wood. Strike after strike. My knees bend with the effort. My breath is so loud in my ears I cannot hear the sound of the blows. Once, the stick misses the wood and finishes the arc of its fall on my bare shin. It cuts. Fresh red blood trickles into the whiteness of my sock, but I do not stop. I have to be certain. I must be certain.

Brendan yells, 'What the hell you doin'? You're not supposed to kill it!'

I strike until the wood splits open. Inside, there is red cloth spreading. Inside, there is a windpipe, like a straw of summer wheat.

Later, in the evening, after Dad has come home from the pub, he yells at me on the verandah.

'Who the hell do you think you are?'

I look up. This giant. Bigger than a red gum. I have to tell the truth or I will go to hell.

'No one,' I say.

He takes *Black Beauty* from his wardrobe and throws it down the lavatory. I see my lovely book there on the top of the pile of filth. I think I might get it out with a piece of wood or the snake wire from the tractor shed. But I can't. I tear off lengths of toilet paper and drop them down the hole until *Black Beauty* is covered up in whiteness.

The night is so still I can hear its heartbeat. A trochee from the night bird by the river. *Mo-poke. Mo-poke.* Through the darkness, past the quiet pools of the Ippinitchie and the windless box trees, it finds me in my room. I feel its cry where my hands are folded in prayer over my chest. Every time I close my eyes, I see *Black Beauty* in the lavatory surrounded by shit.

The moon lights the white lace of my curtain silver-grey, the colour of an overcast sky. The folds of lace fill slowly with the night breeze, until it is thin and round, the shape of an old woman's arm. Mum said Dad did it because he was *cross*. I stick my feet out from under the sheet. I am fevered. In the dark of my room, the body of Jesus glows green on his cross. He is the shape of a t. The shape of a bird. Flying.

I stare at him thinking of the nails going through his hands, and the sticks hitting his wings. Jesus fell with the cross three times. The rosella fell. Black Beauty fell to his knees on the stone. Uncle Albie and Uncle Charlie fell. The fallen. The fall:

To thee do we cry poor banished children of Eve ...

My heart is filled with feathers. Dry as a mopoke.

I dream I see two angels standing on the big branch of the box tree by the barn. Their wings are partly closed. A breeze scented with roses lifts the rounded feathers on their breasts. They are wearing blue saddles, the colour of a kookaburra's wing, and have golden bits in their mouths. Jesus watches from the bore tank where he's walking on water.

I wake up sneezing. I pull on the light cord and do not switch it off for a long time, because I cannot get rid of the picture in my head of the angels wearing saddles and the way they looked at me out of bloodstained eyes.

Kristyn says, 'I understand now.'
'What do you mean?'
'The look on your face when we stood under the cloud of galahs.'

I pour myself a glass of cream and whiskey liqueur. I put it to my lips. It is her skin. I feel the wanting in my thighs. What will become of this chaos of longing?

———

I am six years old, alone in the dark of the verandah, and I see the full moon rise up from behind the wheat field on the hill. At first, there is just a small arc of white light, and I pretend it is a flying saucer resting on the horizon. It is Uncle Martin's spaceship from *My Favourite Martian*. Uncle Martin can't go home to Mars because his ship has crashed to earth and is broken. Sometimes it seems like he has found a way to get home after all, but something always happens to keep him here.

The moon is now full like a perfectly round balloon floating in the sky. When I turn to go, I see that the dark world of the farm is painted with the glow of silver. Everything seems suddenly clear and beautiful. I jump off the verandah and skip out singing past the orange trees to the box tree by the barn where the leaves are white-tipped and shining as if they were made of tinsel. And the moonlit air is scented, a deep amber scent of sweetness. Every breath fills me up with that sweetness. And the sorrow, the wild sparks and my unshed tears are pressed deeper and deeper into the black hole of my heart where they crack and burst. And I dance until the dust and dirt fill my sandals.

As I turn off my bedside lamp, I hear the humming of silver coming through my open window. I feel like a butterfly with warm wings is flying inside my heart. I can't wait for tomorrow to come.'

Kristyn asks, 'What was the sound?'

'The crickets singing in the grass. But I didn't know that. I thought I was listening to music coming from the moon.'

'Everything you described seemed so magical.'

'It was the first day I met Tania Pepper.'

The morning is hot, and leaves shed by the sugar gums are wind-thrown across the playground of the school. Beyond them, near the gate, a perfect row of plantation pines form bars of shadows falling across the yard. In the car beneath their cool darkness Mum gives me my school case. Inside is a blue plastic water bottle and matching lunch box. There is a pencil case shaped like a tube made of pink plastic. On the end of each pencil, my initials CN are written in biro where Aunty Nell sliced out the wood with a razor blade.

In the next car, the Crighton girl is bawling. Betty Crighton holds her by the arm and is trying to pull her out of the car, but she refuses to let go of the steering wheel.

'You're making a scene, Agnes,' Betty says. Her hand smacks against the girl's bare leg. As I slide towards the car door, my legs stick to the vinyl seat. A final resistance.

'Be brave,' Mum whispers.

Two pencil pines tied with wire arch over the front gate and are humming with summer flies. On the right-hand side there is a hollow in the tendrils covered with white web. I know there is a spider devil sitting in there with dark fangs waiting. I look back to Mum.

Mum mouths, 'Make me proud.'

I run through the gate. The corner of my new school case screeches against the post cutting into the plastic. In front of me, a tall thin girl with black hair is skipping. Her skin is the colour of black jade.

'How-come-you're-not-cry-ing?' she says, blowing out every word like it's a birthday candle.

'I don't know.'

'Every-body cries-one way-or a-nother-at first.'

'Mickey says I'll get the cane. Will I?'

'Yeah-when-you're-bad. I-get the cane-every-Friday.'

'Are you bad on Friday?'

She stops skipping and tosses the rope over her shoulder.

'Nah, I get it just in case I was. Do ya want a piggyback?'

'What's that?'

She bends down, her arms at her sides. Her hands curl into shapes like stirrups.

'Put your arms around my neck and hop on. Quick, Mr Henry is gonna ring the bell in a sec. I'll show ya 'round.'

I put down my case. As we take off, my cheek rests against her shoulder.

'There's the long-drops,' she says. 'That's the girls' there. Don't go in the boys', it stinks like a dead cat. Here's the rosemary hedge, and the school garden. We sowed peas and beans in there last year. Duck!' The leaves of the apricot trees brush against our hair. 'Over the garden seat ... and back we go. There's the stuff for you little kids: the see-saw, and the swing you sit on like a bike, and over there is the stuff for the big kids, but stay away from there or you'll get into trouble.'

She tilts her hip so I can get down.

'What's ya name?'

'Cassie Noble. What's yours?'

'Tania Pepper.' She points to the asphalt yard. 'When the bell rings, go over there, at the front by the yellow line. You little kids start there. I'm bigger so I'm near the back.' She picks up her skipping rope. 'I gotta put this away before the bell. See ya.'

I watch her run off into the morning shadows and the open door of the school. I pick up my wounded case and wait for the first strikes of the bell.

Agnes Crighton wets her pants during the roll call when Mr Henry says her name.

Beverly Crighton puts up her hand, 'If sir pleases, I'll get the mop bucket.'

'Exemplary,' he says, smiling. He tells her to draw a star next to her name on the pin-up board by the window. All the students' names are there. Mr Henry says the student with the most stars at the end of the term will get a special prize.

At the back of the schoolroom two new books are open on a table. *The Cat in the Hat* and *The Water Babies*. Mr Henry says the two grade ones, Agnes and me, can look at them while he teaches sums to the older girls and boys. The books are covered with thick plastic. On the cover of *The Cat in the Hat* I draw the cat with my finger, watching the colours smear in the bubbles of air trapped beneath the plastic.

At lunchtime, in the shade of the apricot tree, Tania and I share the apple from my lunch box.

She says, 'You can climb this tree when you're bigger.'

'I'm not allowed to climb trees. Only boys climb trees. Mickey says so.'

'Nah. Watch this,' she says, and quickly she steps up the tree trunk and disappears among the canopy of green leaves. 'You can't see me now, can ya?'

I giggle, 'No. Are you invisible like Uncle Martin?'

She jumps down beside me, laughing. I have never heard a laugh like that before. It sounds like running water in the Ippinitchie after the first of the season's rain.

She says, 'Found an apricot up there.'

'Can I have it?'

'If you say you're my friend. Then you can have it. Go on. You have to say it.'

'Alright,' I say. 'You're my friend.'

She hands me the apricot and kisses me on the cheek.

When Mr Henry says *Tania Pepper* in roll call, there is no answer, just a hole there instead. Beverly puts up her hand and says Tania has the measles and won't be back for a week.

Outside, at recess, the older girls gather under the trees collecting handfuls of pine needles.

'Can I play?' I ask.

'You're not allowed in here,' Beverly Crighton says. 'You've crossed my wall. Can't you see my wall?'

'No. Where is it?'

'There.' She points to a line of heaped pine needles. 'You're treading on it.'

'I didn't see it.'

'Maybe you're blind.'

Megan Cunningham joins them.

'Or deaf and dumb like a dumbo,' Megan laughs.

In the light of the pines their faces look green.

'Who do you think you are, crossing my wall?' Beverly says.

'No one,' I say.

'You'll have to pay now for your sin or you'll go to hell.'

'What do I have to do?' I say.

Beverly pulls open the press-stud of her pocket. She pulls out a brown glass bottle with a black screw top.

'Drink this. Then you'll be one of us. I'll count to ten.'

I take the bottle and put it to my mouth and swallow.

'That's poison,' Beverly says. 'You're going to die. It takes three days to work. You're gonna die on Thursday.'

I am preparing to die. I hold Tiges on my lap and say goodbye. I wrap my arms around Sammy. He smells like the dead sheep he's been rolling in. He pulls on his kennel chain and sniffs the north blown air, scented with smoke from a distant fire. His tail stiffens. He whines, turns, snaps at a fleabite on his rump, and shoulders into the cool dirt. He watches an ant crawl across a pebble by his nose before he closes his eyes. I put my magic bag of knucklebones in the red gum by the river. I want to say goodbye to Tania Pepper, but there is no Tania Pepper.

I can hear them chanting as I walk alone through the playground. Megan Cunningham and Beverly Crighton are sitting on the log-swing facing each other. They are in perfect rhythm, one clap of their own hands and one clap against the other's hands.

My mother said I never should
Play with the gypsies in the wood

If I did, she would say
Naughty girl to disobey.

I want to be able to do that. Chant in rhythm. No, that's not it. Not quite. I want a game that can't be played on my own.

I am by the cattle trough after school, crouched near the barbed-wire fence. Behind me, the worn ground in the cowshed is lined with wild oats, all with their long thin necks broken. Some are already halfway to dust. By the cattle trough the ground is brown like gum moths, and hollowed with cattle hooves. Some of the hollows are holding tiny mirrors of water with the sky in them. At the end of the trough, I hold down the float so water springs from the pipe, cold and silver on my hand and in my mouth.

Mickey yells out from the stable yard, 'The dentist'll get ya.'

I tell myself I cannot hear him for the water. I know this is a lie.

I could be in the kitchen with Mum helping her bake a jam roll and sponge cake for the supper for the Tennis Association meeting. But there are dishes to wash and wipe and put away. Piles of dishes. And hard-to-clean cake tins and oven trays. I run to the barn to hide from Mickey, and crouch low between the wheat bags where it smells of dust and mice droppings. I hear his footsteps on the wooden floor. I hold my breath and concentrate hard to make myself invisible.

'He'll tie you down in a big chair and prop ya mouth open with a stick like the one Mum uses for the clothes line and he'll pull out ya teeth with a pair of pliers.'

I close my eyes and put my hand over my mouth so the pliers can't get me.

'I'm gonna lock ya in here with the rats.'

I hear him click the door.

In the smouldering dark of the barn, I rise trembling. I turn the door handle, and push. The door won't move. I push harder. I call out through the broken window, 'Mum! Mum!'

I know Mum can't hear me above the whir of the mixmaster, Mum's cake mixture folding, folding, layer upon layer. It is a long time before she switches it off and hears me.

'What's wrong?' she calls.

'Mickey's locked me in!'

She opens the door.

'It's not locked.'

'I tried it and it wouldn't open.'

'Well, you couldn't have tried very hard.'

'He locked me in, Mum.'

'The barn door hasn't got a lock. You were probably just pushing the wrong way. I honestly can't believe you called me out of the kitchen just for this.'

I remember the baby rabbit Mickey caught last summer. He put it in a cage that he had built from offcuts and wire netting. One night, when he was at football practice, I decided to set it free, but when I lifted up the door of the cage, the rabbit didn't move. It just sat there folded into itself and shaking, terrified of the open door.

Cousin Teddie's ute pulls up by the gate. Uncle Hopper is on the back sitting on an empty wheat bag, his wooden leg squeezed between tins of honey.

Teddie says to Aunty Nell, 'We're a bit later, Mum, than we'd wanted. Uncle Hopper here forgot to hang on to his hat coming down Chinaman's Creek and it flew off. We had to go back and look for it.' He looks down at me as the ute door opens with a groan. 'I've got the honey for you, young Cassie.'

'That door needs some attention,' Hopper says.

'So does my bank account, but it's not gettin' it either,' Teddie laughs. He says, 'So how are you, cousin Cassie?'

'Mickey says the school dentist is going to pull out all my teeth.'

Hopper laughs a slow, 'He ... he ... he. That dentist'll drill holes in ya cheeks so when ya have a drink a water it'll pour outta ya like you're a fountain.'

'You've got the devil in you, Uncle Hopper,' Teddie says.

'Nah, you see I was born with just one nostril,' Hopper says. 'The school dentist put the other one there with his drill.' He slaps his hip and roars.

Aunty Nell says, 'Now stop it you two! You're scaring the living daylights outta her.'

'Don't fuss now, Mother,' Teddie says. 'She knows we're only teasin'. If we were bein' sensible, we wouldn't be laughin'.'

I say, 'Mickey says the dentist will use pliers.'

'You don't want to believe everything you hear,' Aunty Nell says. 'But when I was your age, we never had no school dentists coming 'round in their fancy trucks like they do now.'

Cousin Teddie sits on the back of the ute with Uncle Hopper, and starts to roll a smoke.

'No good hurryin' when Mother's got a story,' he says.

Aunty Nell says, 'Back in them days we had to make the most of it, toothache or not. A bitta brandy if it got too bad, that's all we had.'

'Hear that, Old Hopper?' Teddie says. 'Is that what got you started on rotgut?'

'Nah,' says Hopper, spitting over the side of the ute. 'Disappointment did that.'

'Anyway,' says Aunty Nell, 'the week after I'd turned twelve, I remember I got gumboils and toothache at the same time. I didn't get a wink of sleep for four days and neither did anyone else because I carried on so much on account of the pain. Then Dad said he'd had enough. He loaded up the buggy with six of us kids and we went off to the doctor twenty miles away. Dad said he had his out at around the same age, and it'd be the best thing all round if I did the same. And besides, there was no way he was gonna put up with any more nights of my hollering and keeping him awake, especially at shearing time.

'Dad went in and told the doctor what he wanted done. Then in I went and that doctor, he had pliers all right and none of that anaesthetic stuff they've got nowadays. I reckon they would've heard me bellowing louder than poor ol' Soursob that winter she lost her calf. But I tell you, that doctor, he pulled out every one of me teeth. One after another.'

'What, even the ones that weren't aching?' Teddie says, lifting his hat and scratching his head.

'He said it was preventative treatment. That I'd never have toothache again,' she says.

'Nothin' left there to ache,' says Hopper.

'Did it hurt?' I ask.

'Hurt? I coulda bitten my way through a four-by-two if I'd had any teeth left to do it with. But it didn't end there. In the other kids all went and had theirs taken out as well. Dad said to us kids, "Better get it all over at once. When it's time to tail the lambs, you go an' do it. You don't go wastin' all spring doin' 'em two at a time." And that's what he told the doctor as well.'

I stick my fingers in my mouth. Looking for gumboils.

'Well, Mother,' says Cousin Teddie, 'I've never heard that one before. I reckon teeth aren't the only thing round here being pulled.'

'So don't you go getting all het up about the dentist,' Aunty Nell says. 'These days they have all sorts so it won't hurt a bit. Not like in my day.'

When they go, I hold up Mum's mirror and shine a torch into my mouth. I am looking for whatever it is that makes me hurt. Not just there in my mouth, but all over.

Mickey has my new basketball that Aunty Nell gave me for Christmas. He dances around me, bouncing the ball.

He says, 'I'm gonna kick it so hard, it'll burst like a galah's head.'

I don't say anything. I can do that now, because I don't feel anything. It is Wednesday, so I am more than halfway to dead.

Mr Henry calls the roll in the morning after assembly.

'Present,' they say in voices which are strange and faraway.

Sometimes in the pause before they answer, I imagine Beverly Crighton and Megan Cunningham are not here. They have been squashed under a tractor like one of the Stanley twins. I look at the inkwell on my desk. I imagine it is a big blue dam. Big enough to hide in.

After lunch we make masks. We blow up balloons and cover them with homemade glue and torn-up strips of old *Flinders Review* newspapers. Layer after layer. It is slippery like frog slime in the Ippinitchie. Later, we paint them and cover them with varnish. Mr Henry uses his pocketknife to burst the balloon trapped inside. He cuts out holes for the mouth and eyes. The older girls make papier mâché ears and a nose. Beverly puts hers on. I wish Tania could see it. Beverly looks like she has a blue pumpkin for a head.

Tania Pepper comes laughing in a red pinafore with her skipping rope.

'Mum thought I had the measles, but it was just a rash.'

'I'm gonna die today,' I say.

'Are ya sick?'

'No the big girls poisoned me.'

'Did they give ya a bottle to drink?'

'Yes.'

'Ya drank it, didn't ya?'

'Yes.'

'It's water. They do that to all the new kids. They did it to me when I came, but I saw them fill it up from the tank. So I put it in my mouth then spat it at them. They told Mr Henry. I got the cane.'

'Does it hurt?'

'Nah. Yeah. A bit. Wanna swap sandwiches? Whaddaya got?'

'Mutton and sauce.'

'Give me one. I've got apricot jam.'

'I'm not gonna die?'

'Nah.'

The taste is both sweet and sour on my tongue.

Tania is kept in at recess to write lines: *I must not laugh in class*, but she'll be here soon. By the radiata pine in the schoolyard a single swing screeches. My feet are tight on the pedals. I hold on while the wind tosses back my head. I close my eyes. I am a galah flying high above the red gums. There is a cry. It echoes out of me. I am rising on an updraft of summer air, over the river, over the hill where the new calves, dazzling red and white, play chasey with each other on the slopes. I can see Sammy tied to his kennel and Tiges dozing on the gatepost. The blue ribbon in my hair loosens and drifts behind me to the ground.

I am riding Black Beauty through the countryside. We dash over an ancient bridge. His shoes ring out high notes on the stone. In a field of bluebells, I am riding, but not one flower breaks under his feet. In the distance is a merry-go-round. A beautiful lady in a flowering red and blue dress waves at me. It's Mary Poppins on her magic horse. Together we canter through a green meadow filled with white daisies. We are singing:

> *A basket of sweet flowers*
> *I will keep just for thee*
> *Wild and white mountain flowers*
> *From the meadow by the sea*

I sing until I am out of breath.

'It's time to go now,' Mary says.

'Don't go, please.'

Mary smiles at me. She is now wearing a blue mantle, Our Lady of Sorrows blue, and I can see through it to her heart. It's crowned with yellow roses and a pink flame.

'See?' Mary says, still smiling, pointing to her heart.

Tania Pepper says, 'Wanna play?'

I open my eyes. Happiness fills me up like air in a balloon. Even the tips of my fingers feel it. I could float away if I wanted to. But I don't want to do that. Not now. Not ever.

The verandah cement is cool under my bare legs. From the screen door comes the scent of baking bread. Above, the wisteria vine drapes over the shoulder of the verandah. With my finger, I trace the shadows of the leaves on the cement. I weave around an ant that crosses the path of my drawing. These ants can hurt. Last summer I sat on one. The welt stung bitter and red for a long time, even when Mum put bi-carb soda on it.

I see Aunty Nell walking back along the path by the orange trees carrying a lettuce from Dad's garden. She sits down on the verandah chair. It's old and green and used to belong to Grandad.

'There might be spiders in there,' I say.

'They'll know better than to try and bite a bit of old mutton like me,' she laughs. 'Now what are you doing out here on your lonesome?'

'Drawing.'

'I don't see any pencil or paper.'

'No, like this on the cement, with my finger.'

'Oh, I see. But why are you only drawing the light bits between the leaves? Why not the leaves, aren't they pretty too?'

'Leaves aren't very exciting,' I say.

'All right then, what about the geraniums? Do you think they're pretty?'

'Mmm, not really. Dad says they grow like weeds 'round here.'

'I want you to try something. Just close your eyes and forget you've ever seen a plain old geranium before. Now, no cheating.'

I close my eyes.

'Now open them, and look over by the verandah post at that geranium in the pot there.'

I open my eyes. In the clay pot with the chip at the top, each geranium petal is trembling with colour, red and orange, then red again as though the fire inside them is the sun burning through every cell. I am watching the light hum in the flowers of the earth. And I know that somehow, from now on, nothing will ever look the same again.

I am hiding from Tania between two daisy bushes, trying not to laugh. The daisy bush on my right has white flowers with soft sappy stems, as if it has grown too fast and not had time to toughen. The fragrance of the flowers is heavy like oil or cloves. A white spider appears on one of the petals. I know if I call out to Tania, our game will end, but I want her to see what I've found.

She lets the spider crawl across her palm. Our hands touch. We are the colours of the sandstone on the cliff face by the river. She tilts her wrist against my fingers, and the white spider steps onto my skin. It has a body like a hailstone. I look, but I can't feel it on my skin. It feels like nothing. But that doesn't mean it isn't there.

I say, 'Do you think it will bite me?'

'Nah, only if you're scared. And you can't be scared.'

'Why not?'

'It hasn't bitten you yet.

We watch it disappear into the white wheels of the daisy petals.

Tania Pepper wraps her skipping rope over her shoulder and we run to the river. The water of the Ippinitchie laughs over the stones, glossed with sunlight and sound. The frogs bellow in their hiding places, but we cannot find them. We tilt our heads in the breaking light of the red gums, catching tadpoles in a Vegemite jar. Some have thick tails turning into limbs. Soon, the tadpoles will journey from the element of water to air, just as we have done.

We call them names. The one with the bulbous body is Beverly. The thin one, dark as a shadow, is Megan. We bend like saplings over the sliding water. The reflections of our faces move and shine as if we are made of liquid like molten glass. Before it cools. Before it takes the shape it will be. Before it breaks.

Time glides across us as a wave. The river moves by, tripping in a blur of foam and light over the warm roots of the red gums burrowed deep into their clay and sand. The school bell rings out the end of lunchtime. We let the tadpoles go. The river carries the imprint of our smiles past the deep pools and the quickened vortices to the sea.

My mother sings 'Galway Bay' in the kitchen while she ices cakes for Father Michael's visit.

'Are we Irish, Mum?' I ask. 'Beverly says I'm Irish. And that my great-grandmother was a monkey.'

Mum is as cold as chilled lettuce. 'There's no Irish in this house.'

I have never seen a priest eat before. The table is covered with the white cloth we usually only use at Christmas. Mum was up at dawn so the baking would be done before Mass. There are feather cakes filled with homemade strawberry jam and fresh cream, golden tipped meringues, jubilee cake sliced and freshly buttered on one side, and teacakes topped with white icing and silver cachous. At the end of the table a big brown teapot steams. It rests on a stand shaped like a diamond, made of bottle tops and crocheted wool. Circling the teapot are six cups and saucers I took from the china cabinet yesterday and dusted with a tea towel. Each has its own freshly polished teaspoon waiting on the saucer like a little silver oar.

'Mrs Noble, this table is surely a work of art,' Father Michael says as he sits down.

Mum blushes and lowers her eyes. I am hoping he won't speak to me, because I want to watch him. I want to see what priests do when they are not in front of the altar, but as Mum is pouring the second pot of tea, he turns to me and says, 'So tell me, are you getting on well with the dear sisters of Saint Joseph?'

'Yes, Father, they come every Wednesday for our lesson,' I say as I bite into the feather cake.

'And what are the little Protestant children doing while you're hearing the truth of Our Lord from Sister Catherine and Sister Dorothy?'

I have to chew and chew before I can answer. I am nervous.

'They have Pasty Smight, Father.' I realise at once, I have used the playground nickname, but I can't take it back or pretend it didn't happen. Brendan and Mickey smirk into their tea.

'Pasty Smight?'

Dad roars. 'She means Pastor Smight, Father.'

'Oh, that indeed is a relief then,' Father says. 'And do the other children, the little Protestant children, ever ask you about your lessons with the dear sisters?'

He takes an enthusiastic bite of jubilee cake.

'Oh yes, Father, all the time. Tania Pepper wanted to know if I was a Christian.'

'I hope you told her you are a Catholic.'

'Yes, Father.'

Father smiles. 'And who is Tania Pepper?'

'My best friend,' I say smiling. 'We play together every day at school. Morning and afternoon recess and all of lunchtime.'

Dad says, 'She's a half-caste staying with the Crightons.'

Mum stirs her tea. The spoon clips against the cup. She says, 'She's exaggerating, Father. Beverly Crighton is her best friend.'

Father says, 'And does Tania Pepper play with you here on the farm?'

'No,' I say, 'Mum won't let me.'

When Father has gone Mum belts me with a wooden spoon. I run over to the box tree by the barn. There are smears of icing still on my hands. I lick my fingers for the last bit of sweetness.

————————

I have time to repair. For two weeks I don't have to think about my past because Kristyn is training with the Flying Doctor Service at Port Augusta. So I can think about a bigger story than my own. I ask myself, *why are we here?* I ask this not as an existential question, but as a literal one. Sarah brought us here. But why did she leave the Burren? I read the books about Ireland that I have borrowed from the Ippinitchie Library, while outside my window there is darkness and stars, and the sound of crickets playing their songs of brushed silver in the grass.

CHAPTER SIX

Music

My people were people of stone. From the clints of *Boireann*, the Burren. The place of stone. County Clare. Ireland. Home was the bleached remains of the hay ropes and the cottage roofs broken in the hunger gales. *An Gorta Mór, The Great Hunger.* A million dead. *Phytophthora infestans* turned the potatoes to soot. But English churchmen said it was sent by God to make the Irish pay for their Catholic sin. On the same road where the people fell, wagons of bacon and grain rolled away under guard to the ports for England. What did the people say as they saw those wagons of plenty pass them by?

Along the limestone drifts, the *caoine*, the crying songs, could still be heard in the grieving and the shifting of the wind. And where the grass pushed through the famine roads built to go to nowhere but across the lines of sorrow for a pound of meal a day. Home was where the bailiff and the battering ram crashed through their cottage walls, and the people walked the dead men's roads and hid in their scalpeens. And they prayed like cursing and they cursed like prayer. My people were people of stone.

There are no photographs of them. No names but one: *Sarah*. Because she was the one to leave. On a boat from Dún Laoghaire amid the cries of those staying behind, the east wind keening through the portal stones of Poulnabrone Dolmen, the hole of sorrows, *What will we do when you've gone?*

I heard her once when I was seven years old. In whispers like white noise, like singing. Like the sound of the wind moving through a she-oak. I didn't know then that points of light breathe their quantum song: now a particle, now a wave, now a particle, now a wave. *Vestigium. Vestigium. Vestigium.*

I dream I am in Ireland. I am hiding in the shadowed corner of a tiny cottage watching a young girl who is standing inside the open door. She has long hair and is dressed in rags. She looks about fourteen. A man in a top hat is at the threshold talking to her. She says to him they cannot pay the rent. She says her mother is sick with fever. She says there is no food for her little sister to eat. She says, 'Have mercy.' He says the only way is to pay him with her body. Or else he'll tumble their cottage and set them on the road to die. The girl turns towards me. I cannot see her face. But she tells me in the silence, there is no one to go to, and no help for them will ever come.

Is her memory in me? In the deep cells of my body? Is this how Sarah reaches through time to touch me, in my dreams?

Hillary has left a message for me on the answering machine.

'Vivienne saw City of Searches last night at the Gov. Apparently, it was their last gig in Adelaide. They're changing their name and moving to LA to try their luck. So you can get your arse down here now and party with me to celebrate.'

The city's air is light and green. In the parkland gardens the lemon-scented gums with their roots deep into the earth soften the noise of the inner-city trade. I see people exiting the shops with shimmering bags, stiff and clean, and frowns upon their faces.

I say, 'I'm trying to work something out, Hillary. What makes a place home.'

We eat takeaway Indian curry on the sands of Semaphore while children with their yellow spades build and destroy and build again their castles beyond the line of the tide.

'That's easy, honey. For me, it's a Clare Valley riesling in the fridge, and his shoes under the bed.'

I look at her, and know I love her. I put my arm around her shoulder.

'Thank you for saving me.'

'You owe me, you know.'

'How can I ever repay you?'

'By coming back.'

———

To the south-west along the Flinders, there is a long curl of cloud like a breaking wave. In the west the sky separates into wings of white and grey that spiral around the mountains, into the gorges and along the blue and purple valleys. Later, they will rise and rest along the high slopes of the hills. Everything shifts and changes. Empires. Villages. Clouds. Once upon a time, the sea was here. It was the southern edge of Australia, a long and curved line shaped like an open wing.

I am thinking about invaders. The colonists here. The British in Ireland. I want similarities. I need similarities. For Kristyn.

An invader comes, because they want land, resources, women, labour or a combination of all four. Rule number one: take what you want. Catch resisters and punish them according to your laws. Just don't call any of this a war. That will legitimise the resisters. They must be seen as criminals and barbarians who hold all law in contempt.

Rule number two: de-humanise the vanquished with stories about their cultural, intellectual and physical inferiority. Deny them resources and encourage self-hatred, and then – this is really important – blame them for their bad behaviour. Such behaviour proves what has been said all along; these people are no better than animals.

Rule number three: teach everyone the invaders' view of history so that anyone who dares to stand up and speak the truth will sound like they're mad.

———————

Her face wakes me in the night. It is the sound of her. I taste her on my tongue. I do not say it, but I hear it a thousand times. The tremble and pull of her name.

It is the same kitchen table where I once did my homework colouring in a picture of Jesus with children on his lap, or drawing Captain Cook taking possession of Eastern Australia in the name of King George. Now, there are three small towers of books and papers about Ireland. About invasion.

We are doing the dishes together after dinner when Kristyn says, 'Have you worked out why your Irish ancestors came here?'

I smile at her, and with an attempt at an Irish accent I say, 'I can't.

I'm just a poor Catholic peasant, and I've not yet learnt to read.'

She laughs and flicks her tea towel lightly against my hip. 'Is that right?'

I feel a shiver run though my body. This makes me blush. I look back down at the dishes in the sink hoping she hasn't noticed and turn on the tap. I do this as if the sounds of water were enough to hide the truth.

'It's the usual story,' I say. 'Ireland was invaded. And the English did what invaders do. They stole the land and murdered resisters. Then they outlawed Catholicism and tried to destroy Irish language and culture.'

'Sounds familiar ... sadly,' she says.

'And that's how the Irish lived for the next couple of hundred years. If my great-grandmother, Sarah, had stayed in Ireland she probably would have starved to death. But those early years in South Australia must have been hard. I don't know what happened, but Sarah ended up in the Destitute Asylum in Adelaide. They trained her to be a servant and she came to the Ippinitchie to work for a local family, the Snaiths. Aunty Nell told me Sarah was allowed one half Sunday off a month.' I dry my hands and open a folder, saying, 'Here, look at this.'

She throws the tea towel over her shoulder.

'This was in *Punch*, one of the English papers during the time of the Great Hunger in Ireland in the 1840s.'

There are two men in the cartoon. John Bull, the Englishman, in his top hat, and Paddy, the Irishman, in rags. He is drawn with the face of an ape.

'Jesus,' she says.

'And it went on.' I open my notebook. 'Here's how the Irish were described in the *Melbourne Review* in 1881 by A.M Topp: "They are, as a race, distinctly inferior, morally, socially, and intellectually, to Englishmen; that they have corrupted and are ever corrupting our political institutions and our public and private morality ... our only hope is to ... assimilate this alien race ..."'

She says, 'Are you sure they're not talking about blackfellas?'

I can't stop. I say without breath, 'And this. Charles Kingsley, the author, in 1860: "I am haunted by the human chimpanzees I saw along that hundred miles of horrible country ... to see white chimpanzees is dreadful; if they were black, one would not feel it so much, but their skins, except where tanned by exposure, are as white as ours ..." We have so much in common. Our cultures have been outlawed and called stone-age, but we're still here.'

'Yes, but your Sarah left Ireland. I'm not waiting for a ship to come to take me to the Promised Land.'

I have been searching so hard and deep for similarities between us. She sees the differences. This does not make me wrong. I feel sad because it makes her right.

'Yes,' I say, 'they are different, and the differences matter.'

In the sitting room by the fire, I say, 'You've never told me your own story.'

'I can't tell you.'

I feel the sting in deep. 'Okay.'

'No, you don't understand. I can't tell you, because I don't know it. My mother, father, grandmother ... I don't know them. I don't even know their names.'

I say, 'I can't begin to understand what that must be like.' She looks into the fire and does not speak. I say, 'But what about you, how did you become a nurse?'

I roll a burning log onto its back with the tongs. Each second of her silence is like a square on the underbelly of the burning wood, pulsing and smouldering in the twilight of the room. I say, 'I'm, sorry. That's your business.'

'Yes, it is.' Soft threads of the bark begin to flame, bursting into little flashes of orange and blue light. She looks at me and says, 'I can't remember the last time someone asked me anything about my life. Where I grew up. What it was like. Are you sure you want to hear about it?'

'Yes, I am.'

She says, 'No questions. I don't want you to ask me anything. Not tonight. And not tomorrow. And not next week. I'll tell you what I feel like telling you and that's it.'

'Yes,' I say. 'I understand.'

I listen as she speaks. Now I see her hands tremble with rage. Now her voice is a whisper as if what she has to say is too painful to say out loud. By the time she finishes her story, the burning wood in the fireplace has turned to flakes of grey and white ash.

She asks, 'What I told you, did you let it in?'

'Yes, Kristyn. I let it in.'

'I've needed to hear someone say that.'

——————

I dream I meet Stephen. Instead of bodies we are two circles of smoky grey, with blurred edges. Exactly the same, but separate. We speak to each other without mouths or language. There is no background. And no scale. So it is impossible to have bearings of space and time. We could be the size of an atom or a star. Whatever it is we exchange in this twilight world, I wake knowing there is something I must do. In a pocket of my wallet is a card creased and soft at the edges from motion and time. The card says, 'Every note I play, I play for you.' I take a saucepan from the cupboard and matches from the woodstove. I don't bother to watch it burn.

Brendan phones from Sydney. He's seen a copy of Dad's will. Dad has left the farm of five hundred acres to Brendan and Mickey and the five acres of Sarah's Garden to me. Brendan tells me to give it back.

'Are you going to fight them?' Kristyn asks.

'They're too big.'

'Too big?'

I close my eyes for a moment, bewildered. 'I can't believe I said that. It was like the little girl in me talking. What I meant was, they're too *determined*, so no I don't think I'll fight them. But I won't give them Sarah's Garden. You know, Kristyn, I still can't believe he's left it to me. I used to go up there all the time when I was growing up. I hoped I'd find something that would show me Sarah had been there. Aunty Nell talked about the keystone from the fireplace having a special design on it that Sarah had carved, but I never found it. I just wanted something to say she'd existed. After awhile, I stopped looking, but I kept going there.'

'Maybe Jack knew it was an important place for you.'

'I never thought he took that much notice of what I did.'

'I heard the way he talked about you when you weren't in the room. He didn't know how to be part of your world. The city. Your work. It was like a foreign country to him. But he said things to me like, "She's done all right for herself down there in the big smoke, the city." Now what that means if you translate it is, *I don't know how to tell her how proud I am.*'

'Or what about this? *She's my daughter and she's done all right. Therefore, I can tell myself I've been a bloody good father, regardless of what she thinks.*'

Across the garden the cold evening air sinks down and settles like frost upon our shoulders.

'I was the one he thought should come back and look after him when Aunty Nell went into the old folks home. Not Brendan. Not Mickey. Me. Because I was the *girl*. He wanted me to just give up everything I'd worked so hard for. But I knew when I left the Ippinitchie for Adelaide when I was seventeen that I wouldn't come back. A door opened, and I wanted it shut behind me. I put myself through my degree with no help from him. I even went to the graduation ceremony on my own. He visited me sometimes, but I never came back here, not even for Aunty Nell's funeral. He was furious. We didn't really speak much after that. He'd phone me at Christmas, but I knew he never forgave me. But I hadn't forgiven him either. For being a fairy tale father. He didn't know what to do with a daughter so he took me into the forest and left me there.'

I sip the tea from my china cup. It is too strong. Rings of bitter notes spread out across my tongue.

From where we are sitting in the garden, I can see the dead limbs at the top of the red gums by the river. Why did a botanist call them *stag-heads*? They must have reminded him of an antelope or a deer. What would the botanist have called them if he'd never seen a stag? We name everything through our knowledge of the world. And me? I have the name of my father, not my mother. My name is not Fahey. It is Noble. What does that mean? I didn't ask for that name.

I say, 'Whether I want to be or not, I'm in a system of inherited property. In the mid 1800s, the authorities subdivided the land

and my family bought it. And it has been passed down through the generations ever since.'

'It was inherited through generations of Nukunu long before that.'

'Yes, but my family bought it in good faith.'

'But not from the Nukunu.'

'No, not from the Nukunu. I don't know how to make that right.'

'Cassandra, I can't give you absolution, if that's what you're looking for.'

'No, I know that.'

'So what will you do?'

'Fight my brothers, I suppose. Try to make that right. I know they are clinging on to the bits of the past that are convenient; the bits that say they deserve more of the pie just because of their gender.'

Beyond the line of ancient hills, the smoke from our little fire rises in twists and spurs into the black space like an arm of a galaxy, as if it were stretching into infinity and back into time.

If I want justice for me, I have to start by calling Mickey. I look in Dad's notebook on the phone table for the number. All day, I pace the house. Planning. Writing notes. Remembering. Planning again. What can I say? What will he say? I decide that I can only plan what *I* will say. That will have to be enough. The skin flushes red on my neck. I go outside for nurture. Through the stratus clouds, pale light washes across the garden. The colours are subtle as if they have been thinned.

At midnight, I ring him in New York.

'Mickey, it's Cassandra.'

'Yeah. It's bloody early. You woke me up.'

'Brendan has told me about Dad's will. How he's left me Sarah's Garden—'

'I can't believe Dad did that. He always said it was all coming to us. What did you say to him when he was sick that made him change his mind?'

'He wrote that will years ago and you know it.'

I tremble. I'm being weak. Still trying to find a way to defend myself against him.

'So are you going to give it back to us?' Mickey says. 'Is that why you've phoned?'

'What century do you think you're living in, Mickey? You're not going to get the whole farm just because you're men. I want Sarah's Garden plus the three blocks of forest along the Ippinitchie to make up an equal third.'

'Jesus Christ. No way. Brendan will never agree to that and neither will I.'

'I'll say this very slowly so you understand. If you don't give me an equal third, I'll challenge you in court and claim everything. I'll win and you'll get nothing.'

'That's what you want, isn't it? Everything.'

'No, I don't. But I do want what's mine.' There is silence. 'Did you hear me, Mickey?'

'Yeah, I heard you.'

'You and Brendan have until the end of the month to agree or I'll start legal action. Is that clear?'

'We'll see about that.'

I hear the phone click.

I vomit into the bath. I look at myself in the mirror. I look like hell. My neck is blotched with scarlet. I say out loud, 'So this is the new me.' And it is. I know now what justice needs. It needs to be spoken. Fought for. Again and again. Even when you may not win.

The night falls in around me until the ceiling of the sitting room darkens and the walls and doors disappear in the blackness. Now there is only a remnant of light from the coals. We need ceilings over us at night. Or the roofs of caves. To secure us from all that infinity just above our heads.

By my bedroom door, the open arms of Jesus still glow green.

I have poached eggs for breakfast on the verandah, looking out across the sky as the swallows feed on insects in the morning air. The phone rings.

'It's me. Brendan.' I hear his rage, 'Why couldn't you leave everything the way Dad wanted? He says clearly in his will the farm is to come to us. Not you. You should have been grateful for what he left you. And now you're blackmailing us into giving you a third.'

'I have just as much claim to the farm as you. Dad's will is unfair. He was stuck in the 1950s. That doesn't mean you have to be. The court will see that, even if you won't.'

'Dad promised us the farm ever since we were boys, and now he's dead you just step in and take it from us. Mickey thinks what you're doing is disgusting. He said, "Typical of the girl to scratch out our eyes to get what she wants." And he's already having a hard time. His wife has left him and his business is in receivership. Some employee took off with half a million. So, I hope you're satisfied. Even if some bloody kangaroo court gives you the nod, it will never make it what Dad wanted.'

'That's not the point.'

'It is to us. You're the one who has to live with what you're doing.'

'I'll manage. So does that mean you'll give me an equal third?'

'You're clearly not going to do the right thing by us.'

I say, 'I am doing the right thing.' I tighten with frustration for slipping into defensiveness. 'There is only one question my lawyers want to know - are you and Mickey going to give me an equal third? The land I asked for along the Ippinitchie?'

'You'll have to wait and see.'

'I'll wait. Until the end of the month.'

It is evening with the tender light of the rising moon. Close by, a wagtail starts to sing. Tonight while the earth glows in moonlight, he will not stop singing. I don't know why. Is he telling other creatures he is lonely, or happy, or is it an anthem of territory?

My longing for her is blue, the deep blue of summer twilight floating at the curved edge of the world. What would she do if she knew? In the night I close my eyes to think of her and I see a shaft of deep blue light shape-shifting into clouds, which spark and soar and burst open into the trembling dark. Then it begins again as a single point of light. A star burning blue. A full stop. I say her name as I go to sleep. The way I used to say a prayer.

———

Kristyn says, 'What do you remember of the week Tania disappeared?'

I say, 'The past is a dangerous country.'

'Yes,' she says.

Mum says, 'They're all saying on the wireless that if they get the votes, Aborigines are going to be counted in the census. Just like us.'

I am sitting on the kitchen floor listening.

Dad opens a bottle of beer and fills three glasses.

He says, 'They reckon it's the only fair thing.'

Mum says, 'Father Michael didn't say a word about it at Mass this morning. And now it's too late. We go to vote on Saturday. I wanted the Church to tell me what to think. How else can I know what to do.'

Dad says, 'Just vote *yes* and forget all about it.'

She looks at Aunty Nell, 'How can Aborigines be counted like us? They're not us ... are they?'

My mother and I are at prayer in the sitting room by the Immaculate Heart of Mary. Her rosary beads are curved so tightly over her fingers the circle breaks. She wraps the rosary back in her hands, kisses the feet of Christ on the cross and whispers, 'What do you want me to do?'

I am carrying Tania's skipping rope as we walk through the schoolyard. Beverly and Megan are playing their hand-clapping game under the pines. They see us coming. Together in perfect rhythm they change one word when Tania and I walk by. One word.

> *My mother said*
> *I never should*
> *Play with the nigger*
> *In the wood*

Tania runs so fast I can't keep up. On the other side of the schoolyard, I find her sitting in the apricot tree by the fence. I can see Tania's legs swinging under the leaves. Her white socks. Her white sandals.

'I can see your undies,' I say. 'They're pink.'

'So?'

'Can I climb up too?'

'It's too high. You'll hurt yourself.'

'No I won't.' I hold on to the rough trunk and pull.

'There's no room for you.'

'Yes, there is.'

My hands slip. Splinters dig into my skin. It doesn't hurt. I pull myself up. Tania is looking the other way.

'Got your skipping rope,' I say.

'Don't wanna.'

'Why not?'

'Cos.'

'Cos what?'

'Just cos.'

I lift the rope from my shoulders and hang it on the branch. Tania turns to face me.

'I wanna go home,' Tania says.

The splinters in my hand start to pulse with pain.

'Like Uncle Martin in his spaceship?' I say. I blow on my hands to make the hurting go away. 'Want half a scone?'

'Nah. Yeah. All right.'

I unzip the side pocket of my dress and pull out a scone. I break it in half and hand it to her. Tania leans over and kisses me on the cheek.

When Mr Henry rings the bell, I slide down the tree.

'Aren't you coming?' I ask.

'Nah,' Tania says.

I run towards the classroom. Before I turn the corner into the playground, I look back at the apricot tree. Tania Pepper's legs are still swinging from under the leaves.

After school, Brendan and Mickey run though the gate towards home. I go to the apricot tree and look up into the green and golden leaves.

'Are you up there, Tania? Are you pretending you're invisible?'

But there is no answer. I sit on a swing in the empty playground. No Beverly Crighton. No Megan Cunningham. No Tania Pepper saying, 'Wanna play?' No Tania Pepper. I fill my hands with pine needles from Beverly and Megan's wall and drop them into the Ippinitchie. As if the river had the power to carry away such a wall.

High above me in the canopy of the pines, the dark bodies of the choughs flit by. White circles flash open on their wings. One cries, a single whistled note falling in a curve of sound towards me, the dead leaves, the rust-coloured reeds and the trembling water of the Ippinitchie. One last time, I go back to the apricot tree.

I say, 'Why aren't you there?'

Kristyn says, 'And that was the last time you saw her?'

I nod. 'And I'm so sorry my mother behaved that way about the referendum. It was shameful.'

'Yes, it was,' Kristyn says. She steps up from the verandah, and says, 'And there was never any sign of Tania again? No clue about what happened that day?'

I feel a cold shadow darkening the pathway into my words. I am not sure how to answer her. I feel the loosening now, the dark coming. What do I do? To get rid of a shadow you either turn on more lights, or turn them all off. One or the other. That's the choice. The black and white of it. More light or less. But which do I choose?

I wait by the gate for Mum to come to pick me up. But she doesn't come.

The light on the hillside above the school hangs in the golden air. I will go home on my own.

My breathing crashes in my head like waves. I hear nothing else. Inside my school case, things rattle as I run as fast as I can, the lunch box with the crumbs of my mutton sandwich, the pencils in their case breaking their leads. My sandals fill with dirt. I hit a rock with my toe. My eyes water, but I do not stop. I have to run faster like the boys. They are bigger because they are boys and boys can do things better. They are not bigger just because they are older. They tell me this when they are being kind. When they see that I need to be taught things. I shouldn't get my hopes up to run as fast as they can. I won't be able to. Ever. My sandals slip on the dirt. I change hands with my school case as I run. I jump over the shadows of the red gum branches as if they were real hurdles.

I slow. My breath softens and the sounds of the bush come back. The whip call of a shrike-thrush cracks open the afternoon air. In the wattle bushes and the grass the invisible heart of autumn hums. Ahead I can see the footbridge across the Ippinitchie, lined and sun-dried grey, and its broken railings no one has got around to fixing. A breeze rustles the dead leaves from the red gums. In a single motion Mickey dives from behind a bush and wraps his arms around my shoulders. I fall backwards on the road. My back slams into the ground. The dirt punches into my elbows. As I fall, that is the sound I hear, my body thumping into the ground. But the sound is distant, like a mopoke call, or pencils rattling in my school case.

'Gotcha!' Mickey yells.

'Hey, not too rough,' Brendan says. 'We don't wanna hurt her.'

When I open my eyes the world is blue and black checked. Somewhere to my left is a bright red light. The sun. But I can't be sure. I know now my head is wrapped in my dress. I struggle, but my wrists are held fast by their hands.

'Let me go,' I say.

'When you stop fightin',' says Mickey. A stone digs into my shoulder blade. Mickey says, 'We won't let ya go while ya keep fightin'.'

My dress over my mouth inflates and shrinks with my breathing. There is silence for a moment. I cannot move my ankles or my hands. Their grip heats against my skin. I stop fighting.

'Let's give her a Chinese burn,' Mickey says.

I don't know what that is, but I know it will hurt so I kick my legs hard against Brendan's grip. He laughs and his fingers tighten around my ankles. Mickey twists my skin between his hands. My right arm screams with pain, pulsing and jerking inwards towards the bone then outwards to the air. My limbs stiffen as if I were dead.

At the gate to Aunty Nell and Teddie's, the sun bursts through the trees, lighting up a patch of prickly pear by the fence.

I say, 'I'll tell Mum, then you'll be sorry.'

'No, we won't,' Mickey says. He stops to pick up a stick, and starts to wave it above his head. 'You'll be the one who'll be sorry. We'll tell her you hurt yourself climbing up a tree.'

'That's not true.'

'Yeah, it is. So tell her if ya wanna, but she'll go crook and belt ya with the wooden spoon. Girls aren't meant to climb trees. Only boys are allowed to do that. That's the rule. Mum said so.'

The stick whirls out of Mickey's hand, spinning like a loose propeller over the fence and into Teddie's dam. The wild ducks rise, flapping their wings to hover in the air before disappearing over the almond trees. I look at the stick sinking and the waves rolling across the water.

At home, I see Aunty Nell in her bright floral dress standing in the vegetable patch. Not moving. Just standing, looking at the ground as if she's lost something. Mum didn't forget to pick me up. She says Mum is in hospital with a sore chest so I have to help cook dinner. I peel potatoes until my fingers hurt. Dad says no school for us tomorrow. We'll visit Mum instead in the hospital.

I don't want any stories from Aunty Nell tonight. I go to bed and read *The Water Babies*, the part where Tom the chimney sweep is punished for eating too many lollies and is suddenly covered in thorns. I want to be like Tom. Covered in thorns. To keep everyone away.

I dream the voices of Megan and Beverly and Mickey are rising and falling around me in chants. I can't tell what it is they are singing, but it is strange and dark like the black night water of the Ippinitchie as it slips over the rocks, and pulls and foams at the bend by the bridge. The sound becomes a shape. Made of pine needles and barbed wire.

'Why were you running?' Kristyn asks. 'In your story, when you were going home from school. You kicked your toe and you didn't stop. Did you see something?'

My head smarts with pain. I look away from her.

'I don't know why I was running.'

And for now, that is the truth. But for how long will I be able to say that?

They are walking, Dad, Brendan and Mickey. I follow behind them carrying a jar with a butterfly inside. Its wings are full of holes, but it keeps flapping them as if it were still able to fly. I'm listening to the sound of footsteps on the linoleum corridors between the wards. Heels click on the wax. It is the cleanest sound I have ever heard. Overhead, the lights are bright, reflecting white fireballs onto the floor. I think it strange my shadow is strong enough to break them in two as I pass.

As we walk by the geriatric ward I see a row of beds with pale yellow coverlets, each containing a white-headed old woman. Some of these women are surrounded in a U shape by adults chatting noisily to one another. The one nearest the door is curled up into her own shoulder as if it were a wing and she were a bird terrified of the light or noise. We meet an old woman wearing a pink dressing-gown and slippers.

'G'day there, Mrs Casey,' Dad says.

Mrs Casey smiles at him and starts to sing:

Catholics, Catholics ring the bell, while the Proddies go to hell.

'That's right, Mrs Casey. That's right,' Dad says.

When they reach a big yellow door, Dad says, 'You kids better wait out here.'

'She's going all right, isn't she?' Brendan asks.

'What sort of bloody question is that?' Dad says. 'Now just you wait here.'

When he has gone through the door, Brendan pinches Mickey's arm. Mickey slaps him on the shoulder. I sit on a chair away from them. I want time with the butterfly in the jar. I wonder if a butterfly can feel in its wings? And when its wings are all full of holes, why doesn't it know it can't fly anymore?

Dad appears back at the door.

'Just the girl,' he says.

As I pick up my jar Dad says, 'You better leave that bloody thing outside.'

I put the jar down on the floor just inside the door.

I think this must be the wrong room. Everything is too big. I look at the woman on the bed who has a tube disappearing up her nose. There is at first nothing familiar about this woman. Her hair is unbrushed and limp against the pillow. And things are out of shape, like my pink cardigan Aunty Nell accidentally tossed into the hot wash last week. When she took it off the clothesline the arms were lopsided and the back had changed into an oblong of bright purple. Everything here is the wrong size. The room is too big. Dad is too small. And Mum is a different shape than I remember.

'You better come here then,' Dad says to me. Dad is leaning over the bed and says, 'She's here. The girl. Brendan and Mickey are outside like a bunch of tomcats pickin' on each other. I didn't wanna bring them in all at once. Be too much for you. I've spoken to Doctor awhile ago. He says you just need to rest up. Get yourself back on your feet. I better go back out there an' see what the boys are up to.'

I am alone in the room with my mother. I watch the hospital gown covering her chest rise and fall with her breath. Mum's mouth moves. She is trying to speak. I lean forward, balancing on my toes so I can reach her. I want to tell her about the Chinese burn.

'Mum?'

I am sitting on the kitchen floor with my back against the wall. The lino is cold this far away from the warmth of the woodstove, but I stay where I am.

'What should I do with the butterfly, Aunty Nell?'

'Everything wants to go on as long as the suffering's not too much. The trick is to know when it's had enough.'

'I saved it from the ants.'

'Yes, I know you did. Just remember next time, even if you are

162

really careful, your touch can kill a butterfly and turn their wings to dust.'

I press my face to the glass jar, and whisper, 'I'm sorry.'

Brendan yells out from the verandah, 'Hey! Come and have a look at this.'

I follow Aunty Nell through the screen door. Mickey is looking upwards, his left hand shielding his eyes. 'Over there.' In the western sky is a tiny dark cross, and behind it is a strip of shining white. 'One of those planes goin' to Sydney,' Brendan says.

'Or England,' Mickey says.

Brendan pokes him in the midriff. 'Yeah? How would you know?' They lock bones. 'Sydney. It's goin' to Sydney,' Brendan says.

'I knew a chappy once who'd been to Sydney,' Aunty Nell says. 'It was during the war.'

A burst of afternoon sun is savage enough to water an unprotected eye, but I can't look away. I am trying to remember every detail so I can tell Tania. Against the wild blue of the sky and the strike of the sun, the jet is transfigured, a cross of limestone white, like a chapel candle.

I am behind the haystack with an empty jam jar and a swallowtail butterfly dying at my feet. On the line of soft green grass watered by the hay-shed roof, it tilts, and overbalances, a tiny yacht in a green swell. I raise my foot and feel the crush beneath the heel of my sandal. Pins and needles of pain dig in. I look down at the brokenness in the grass. The red circles on the wings are still. I look at my hands. The butterfly is my obverse; the wing prints on to my fingers. An opalescent dust. High above the jet trail bleeds, like ink into blotting paper. Like Vermilion Red lipstick on to skin.

The late afternoon sunlight through the kitchen windows splits the room into blocks, like a giant stone cracked by time and pressure along fault lines of light and dark. Dad is in the sitting room talking to Dr Squire on the telephone and somewhere outside Sammy is barking. Dad has his right hand over his ear.

'No, Doctor,' he says, 'I don't have any questions to speak of.'

I try to be quiet as I sneak past Dad, but sometimes trying makes things worse. I drop my jar on to the floor. He turns around to me. His face is bloated as if he were in a rage. Because I expect something bad to happen, my body won't bend for me to pick up the jar. I will get a belting one way or another. Instead, he turns and walks slowly to the shelf above the fireplace. His hand stills the pendulum of Mum's wind-up mantel clock. The ticking stops at five minutes to five.

He says to me, 'That was the doctor. Your mother ... she's gone. Nell'll get your dinner.'

I wake up just after midnight as the wind comes howling cold along the hills, shaking the orange trees and tipping over an empty watering can on the verandah. Sammy rushes out of his kennel and barks, but the sound is carried away into the night. The moonlight is thick in my room so I know it will be easy for the dark eyes of God to see me. Sister Dorothy says the eyes of God are everywhere. They see everything. All the wicked sins of little girls that make Jesus suffer so. They saw my touch kill the butterfly. And they even saw my biggest sin. That I touched Mum in the hospital when she was sleeping. Just the back of her hand with my little finger. I didn't think it would hurt her. I didn't think it would count. Did I wipe away the colours of her wings?

I say to Aunty Nell, 'Where's Mum?'

'She's gone, sweetheart,' Aunty Nell says. She tries to hug me, but I don't let her. I'm not used to anyone being that close to me anymore. Only Tania.

I hear my dress tear as I bend under the barbed wire. There is a place on my back already warming with blood, but for now it doesn't hurt. The sheep tracks meander across the slopes towards the ranges. The hillside is soft with new grass, textured like kangaroo fur. It's a long way up there to Sarah's Garden, further than I've ever been. But I'm going to find her. And ask her what to do. About Mum.

Above the red gums by the Ippinitchie a cockatoo screams. Dad says they call like that when they are lost. The sound echoes along the shoulder of the hillside. My sandals slip against the ground. Only Dad and the boys have boots to walk the farm. My shadow climbs in front of me. I pretend it's Tania showing me the way.

I lean over to rest with my hands on my knees. This is higher than I've ever been. I see a copper lizard, the autumn sunlight polishing its back, and a damask and white feather like a flag on a stalk of grass. I give it to the wind.

On the edges of the sheep track the last of the spring grass is stiff and scratches against my skin, leaving little white marks on my legs. I rub my ankle, loosening a thread from my sock the length of an eyelash. Mum will find it next washing day and sew it back with invisible thread. She'll be back by then.

I pass sheep fossicking among the fresh new grasses and rosettes of Salvation Jane. I forget to watch where I'm putting my feet, and kick my toe against a ploughshare half buried in the dirt. I stop while the pain pulses through my foot. In a dead tree in a gully, a crow glistens in the sunlight. *Aaar ... aaar ... aaar*. Its moans are as sad as the wind. Dad says you can't shoot a crow. Not because you can't, but because you can't.

He says, 'If you aim a stick at it making out it's a gun, it'll just sit there laughin' at ya. But by Jove, if you point a rifle at it, it'll be off all right.'

'How does it know which is which?' I wanted to know.

'Hell, I don't know. You'll have to ask the crow that.'

So I ask. It looks at me and laughs, a black liquid laugh that oils the brisk autumn air. Some things here are secrets, real secrets like those of crows and men.

Dad tells the boys special stories. And there is nothing on the farm they're not allowed to see. Mum and Dad don't want me to see sad things. But I have anyway. Things like the eyeless head of a sleepy lizard, a baby bird still wet with egg slime kicking against a thousand ants.

One morning, I overheard Dad talking to Brendan on the verandah. 'Most of the chooks are gone. Tell your mother to keep the girl inside til we've cleaned up the mess.'

When Mum let me out, I ran down to the chook house to look for Mrs Hen and the four little chickens. Mum and I had named them John, Paul, George and Ringo. They weren't there. I sat by their water bucket for a long time. Wondering.

'Where are the Beatle chooks, Mum?'

'They've gone,' she said. 'Now, set the table like a good girl.'

To my right is a dead sheep, an island, white and ragged in a sea of green grass. The ribs are open like a broken birdcage. I pick up the skull. It's cool in my hands. A pearl spider the size of a sixpence appears in the eye. The skull falls to my feet. I roll it over with my sandal. There might be a centipede or a legless lizard in there too.

The spider shrinks, pretending death on the grass. I want to squash it for having scared me. I don't. Mickey says all things are stronger when they are dead, just like Jesus. If I can be like that, it will be alright to die.

I pick up the skull again and this time hold it in front of me, in the same way that Father Michael holds up the chalice at Mass. I look through the magic holes that once were eyes. I see I am close to a city of ants. They are purple, and are busy carrying little dark stones to their nest. An ant crawls onto my sock. I put down the skull, flick the ant to the ground, and hurry away.

Now the crest of the hill rises steeply. I walk sideways to keep my balance over a tangle of dead branches. I pass a stump with an avalanche of red dirt on the leeward side, and look ahead to a cliff line of jagged rocks. As I stop to rest my legs between hard breaths, I hear the wail from the she-oaks. I step through the opening in the rocks. The wind slaps my face making my hair whip at my eyes. They start to tear. In front of me, there is nothing. There is no house. No chimney. There is only a tumble of broken rocks, a stand of seven she-oaks and a single rose briar.

Why isn't she here?

Under the thin shadow of the trees, I sit on a stone shaped like the clouds that form in summer above the ranges. I angle my head to the wind the way Sammy does when he's chained to his kennel. In the forest towards the ranges a chainsaw snarls. High above me I see the black *t* of a wedge-tail. It circles once, twice, then disappears on a rising current into the blue. I watch until my eyes hurt from too much light. I want to be up there. Not flying. But vanishing.

It is silent now the wind has calmed, and I am alone. Mum isn't anywhere, is she?

'Why? Why?' I bellow.

I pick up a fallen stone from the ruin of Sarah's cottage. I rub the stone until my hand bleeds.

I hear a noise like whispers. I can't tell if it is a single voice speaking over itself, or many different voices. But the sound feels *travelled*, the way light looks through dust or rain, without clear lines, when part of it has been refracted away, and diffused. I can't tell where it's coming from. But it's here.

I listen to the sound and put down the stone.

It is morning, and Dad is in his suit and tie. He smells like laundry soap.

'You're staying with Mrs McKenzie for the day. Teddie and Nell will get you later and bring you home. After it's over.'

Moira McKenzie says, 'I'll look after you, dear.'

I eat buttered slices of jubilee cake while she pours me cups of milky cocoa in her best rose china. I know it is her best because the saucer doesn't have any cracks. She takes me outside to a tyre swing under the peppercorn tree. She gives me little pushes on my shoulders until I am higher from the ground than I've ever been.

'There now, isn't this fun, Cassie?' she says.

I know I should be smiling because I like the feel of flying on the swing, but what I want is the scent of Vermilion Red lipstick and the sound of my mother's voice singing *Tobar Bride* in front of the mirror.

———————

Dad says to me, 'Just you tomorrow to school. I need the boys this week on the combine to get the wheat in. Another few days away won't hurt them.'

I wait for Mr Henry to call Tania Pepper's name. For Beverly Crighton to raise her hand saying, 'Please, sir, but Tania Pepper is sick with the measles.'

I wait, but he does not say her name. And Beverly does not raise her hand. I want to know where she is. I want to tell her things.

At recess I walk over to the edge of Beverly and Megan's pine needle wall.

'Has Tania got the measles?' I ask.

'Tania who?' Beverly says.

'Tania Pepper.'

'Who's that? Your pretend friend?'

'Cassie has a pretend friend. Pretend friend,' they chant together.

The air I breathe is frost, so cold it burns.

I tremble as I say to them, 'Where is she?'

Beverly Crighton says, 'Mum says your mother is in heaven, with Jesus.'

But that's not what I meant. I want to know where Tania is. But now I cannot ask again, because all I feel is grief like a razorblade scraping at a sting in my skin that will never come out.

——————

We sit outside on the verandah. Seeds of sunlight sow themselves on the grass lit by rain.

'What will you do if you win against your brothers?' Kristyn asks. 'Go back to Adelaide?'

'I suppose if I do win I could sell my share of the farm and have enough to pay off my mortgage at Tower Court. That would give me time to look for another job. But I don't know if I want to do that. I can't bear the thought of selling.'

'Don't sell then. Stay,' says Kristyn.

'I suppose I could teach art again. If I sold Tower Court and continued to lease the land to Col, I'd probably have enough to build a little place on Sarah's Garden. I could live here in Dad's house until it's ready.' The possibilities come rushing in on a rising tide. 'The stone's already there just waiting to be put back together. And I remember Aunty Nell telling me that when she lived there they had a big underground rainwater tank. Dad filled it in years ago. The timber roof was falling in, but under the rubble it would still be there.'

I hear myself and I stop. This is not a life. I have a ruin. I have a memory of a place I once loved when I was a child, because it was a place to grieve. And now, I'm talking as if I could make it my home.

'Have you been up to Sarah's Garden since you've come back?' Kristyn asks.

'No,' I say.

'You live on this bloody verandah, Cassandra. It's like a margin separating you from everything that matters. When was the last time you even ventured beyond the house paddock?'

'I don't know. Not since I left home.'

Kristyn reaches for my hand. 'Come on. Sarah's Garden. I want you to take me there.'

It is the noise of a midwinter's afternoon. The galahs crying for home, a wattlebird rising on silent currents of air feeding on invisible things. We walk the sheep track along the crest of the ridge. It is less steep than I remember. To the right, about halfway along the ridge, is a giant blue gum Great-Grandfather never got around to grubbing. It's the only one he left in a paddock of sixty acres. Not because it was too big and he didn't have the heart to cut it down. The truth was he'd run out of puff.

As we reach the summit, the wind turns towards us, scented with eucalyptus and pine. In every direction the colours fold and rest against one another. The dark shimmer of pine forest, the pale green of the crops, and the shining bushlands of blue gum and box. And beyond, the sea blue of the Flinders.

'It's overwhelming,' Kristyn says. 'It's too much to take in.'

'That's the Ippinitchie down there in the ribbon of river reds. Over there,' I point to the range, 'at the second curve of the river, is where Sarah first lived with her husband Michael before she built here.'

I turn to face east. 'You can't really see from here, but out from the road that leads into the town is where my grandmother Mary lived. Aunty Nell's sister.'

Halfway along the summit of the hill, there is a she-oak tree in a nest of granite rock and fallen stones.

I say, 'This is what's left of Sarah's Garden. Just a pile of stones. But I've always believed Sarah is here, looking out for me. That's what Auntie Nell used to tell me in her stories. And I believed her. This place inspired the last painting I ever created.'

Kristyn steps closer to the she-oak. The trunk is etched with vertical lines and is dark like charcoal.

'I don't know why Dad left this one.'

'I can't believe he'd want to cut them all down.' Kristyn touches the trunk with her open palm. 'Oh it's so beautiful,' she says.

'They grow where nothing else will survive. Then they stand and sing about it. *I'm here. I'm here. I'm still bloody here.* Listen Kristyn. Just listen to it.'

The breeze howls softly through the branches. It's the sound of breath moving through a mouth shaped for a whistle or a kiss.

I say, 'The botanist who named it must have been a poet. He thought the leaves were like the feathers of a cassowary. That's why it's called casuarina.'

Kristyn smiles and says, 'It sounds a bit like Cassandra, don't you think?'

We sit, facing the western sun. I say, 'Do you know what happened when the Europeans first came and saw these trees? They noticed the timber was similar to the great oaks of England, but inferior. So they called them she-oaks.'

'Christ! Is that true?' she says. 'It's lucky beliefs have nothing to do with the truth.'

'No, but people act as if they do. They kill for them. Die for them. And there's no way to fight against someone's belief.'

'I think you can with science. That's why I love anatomy. It's not about belief.'

'Does that mean you think there's never any room for miracles?'

'What do you want, Cassandra? Just look around you. The sky. Here. This stone. This grass. Everything is a miracle. This is a day when I don't have to watch somebody dying. Instead, I'm here in this magnificent place with you. That's a miracle.'

Kristyn is standing now with the sun behind her. The afternoon light is shining on her hair.

'So, are you ready?' she says.

'For what? I don't know what you mean.'

'Just tell me. Are you ready? Do you want to find out if you belong here?'

'I don't know. You're making me nervous. What do I have to do?'

'Take off your clothes.'

'What for?'

'Because if you want this place to feel like home, you have to feel it. With your skin. I'll sit over there with my back turned behind the rocks.'

'What do I do?'

'Feel the ground with your body. To do that, first you touch it with your eyes. If you want to love the land you have to look first, then look again but more deeply, then you feel it with your hands. Feel the pulse there in the ground. Then feel it with your skin. And then just see what happens. I'll be here if you need me.'

My fingers touch first a drift of fallen she-oak leaves at my feet. They look like the needles of a pine tree, but are softer, longer. I see there are parallel lines and joints of raised gold along each leaf. They have no scent. I am kneeling now on the leaves. They are soft like string.

'Touch it with your shoulder,' Kristyn says, the sound of her voice travelling to me from behind the ruin of stones. 'Rub the ground with your shoulder. You are scenting yourself with the land. Then lie down. As it touches you, the land is scenting you.'

I look for enemies, ants and spiders, but find none.

'I can't do this.'

'What do you feel?'

'I'm afraid.'

'What are you afraid of?'

There is a gasp, brief and so sharp-edged, it cuts into my throat. The words tumble, a ruin of stones no longer able to hold the last of its shape.

'It won't want me.'

I am on my knees trembling. I turn and lower myself slowly onto the leaves, unfolding my back, my shoulders and neck until I am lying on the ground.

'Ask. Ask the ground then. Ask it if it wants you,' Kristyn says.

I am in the long space now between afternoon and evening where the song of the earth is a hum, slow and languid like a string touched and played. I'm kneeling on the ground at Sarah's Garden, my long white shirt now half undone. This is the place where the plates of life move up, across, or slip aside. It is called a fault line. Yes. But it isn't a fault. This is the line where mountains have been born. And from the shifting rocks surges a quiet power into the nerves of my feet, into my thighs and through the cage of bones around my heart. Can I say it is fire?

I am about to close my eyes, then I hear a voice too calm to be my own. Where has it come from, this voice? This calm voice from inside the ancient shifting ground of my body?

Kristyn, can you please come here?

Two women are standing under the she-oak. Kristyn and me. The breeze hums and sighs through the leaves, the cassowary feathers of the genus casuarina.

'I want to ask you something,' I say.

'Sure.'

'You may laugh at me.'

'Probably not.'

'Kiss me,' I say. 'I want you to kiss me.'

She moves towards me. I don't know what she'll do. She has never been this close facing me. In the darkness of my closed eyes the kiss comes slowly, a gentle press of sun-warmed silk against my lips, the shock of softness, like the mirror of shallow water at the edge of the dam.

Kristyn draws back and I open my eyes. We look at each other. Am I asking? Is she? The next kiss comes quickly, and then the taste of her breaks open like honey in my mouth. The embrace between us now comes with such force, my shoulder slams backwards against the trunk of the she-oak. Now Kristyn's mouth is on my throat. Together our breathing sounds like fabric tearing. Then in one motion Kristyn's hands push down against the front of my shirt. The buttons spill open. One tears and rolls away. Kristyn pauses for a moment as she looks at me. Truly looks at me. She moves forward and I feel her tongue against my neck, then my breast. A sob rises up through my body, the sweet hurt of all these months of longing. I lean forward, aching for her mouth. I find it, a kiss so deep I feel like I'm shedding light.

I am so close now to falling, I arch backwards against the tree until I feel her fingers slide across my thighs, our mouths still touching. My fingers bend into her neck, and my head falls back against the she-oak, grazing my skin. I cannot feel the drop of blood falling against the bark. But I know it's there. So tightly I hold her, we slide down together on to the leaves. My body still trembling, I am sighing into her neck. Under the red blazed leaves of the she-oak, we lie together, looking only now into each other's eyes. We are breathless, shining.

She lifts my shirt away from my shoulder. My skin opens to the warm air of the breath and touch of her. She draws my shape with the touch of her mouth; the warm pearl of my collarbone, the curve of my hip. I feel the iron softness of her limbs as she holds me. I shiver and burn.

The she-oak sings in the evening breeze that rises from the Ippinitchie across the green grass of the paddocks to where I wake now to her body loving me. A wind that cannot cool our skin. Gently we go past the wounds and scars into the hollows of each other, as if we were each carrying a lamp there that flames in the wind, but does not go out.

I open my eyes to see her hand rising slowly to my face. Her fingers and palm press softly against my cheek. She touches me as if I am sacred.

'Oh, Cassandra,' she says.

Her tears are in my mouth. For a long time there are no more words, only breath and touch and stars.

How can this be?

The curve of her waist is between my thighs, the sweat on her breast is on my tongue.

In silence we gather wood and light a fire. By its light we sleep in the song of each other. I have used my breath to start a fire in winter when the wood is green or damp from sudden rain. I have seen a white spark running along the hair of the bark and the flame come in a sudden burst of yellow and blue. When her breath touches my skin I feel like that. And the coals at the end of the night fire when each line in the wood, each textured square is alive, a throb of colour, a fire with no flame. But still there is the flare into the dark, as if each coal were a light with infinity to burn.

There is a scar on her hip shaped like a rainbow.

The bones around her heart are as strong as metal roads.

———

I have fifteen minutes before she's here. I pull a chair close to the fire for her and sweep the hearth. In front of Mum's dressing table mirror I brush my hair. I put on a different jumper. I take it off and put on another. I put on lip-gloss. I rub it all off. I brush my hair again. It's now alive with static. I hear it spark.

The moonlight is a soft burn through the window, just strong enough for shadows.

She sits at the edge of the bed, her back to me, and begins to undress. I lean over and curl my arms around her shoulders.

Into the silver dark, I say, 'You are holding on.'

'What will happen if I let go?' she says.

'Do you want to know?'

The shadow of the unlit lamp falls across her face.

Her skin opens like water and lets me in.

The moonlit pollen of her scent spreads over my thighs, my hair and in my eyes. We sleep with her body curved into my arms, my hand upon her brow.

In the morning I say, 'This is the closest I've been to home.'

The yellow thornbill resting in the sultana vine is not the same one that was here when I left all those years ago, when I boarded the Bluebird train at Gladstone for Adelaide with dreams of becoming an artist. And the choughs by the river are seeing me for the first time as they look up from feeding in the grass and leaves with their eyes shining like red glass. And me. My skin. This time. This year is not the same. This time it is beneath her touch.

I say, 'Do you know where I go when I'm holding you like this?'

'Into my body.'

'Do you know how I get there?' Her eyes are glossed and deep like amber. Not the amber of resin, but of sapwood, the crystal that fills wounds. I say, 'Through my own soul.'

I will replace my broken *Sorrows of the King* with *Music*. Matisse painted it in 1939. Two women. One is dressed in gold, the other in blue. The one in blue is playing a guitar. The guitar has strings. There is an open sheet of music in front of her. Yes, I will hang that on the wall instead. I just don't know which wall.

My body is becoming transparent. Now she can see everything.

She says, 'You know something, don't you? About the day Tania disappeared. There's something you haven't told me.'

'Why do you say that?'

'I can feel it in your body. And bodies don't lie.'

I press my lips together to keep the cry inside. I don't want to feel it cutting its way upwards in my throat. I don't want the sound of it here in this space I've made for us. She turns her body away from me. This is the risk, isn't it? Truth always threatens to break us.

I say, 'I can remember why I was running so hard along the road the day Tania disappeared. Why I didn't stop when I hit my foot against the stone. What I don't know, Kristyn, is how long I've known. That's the truth.'

I am seven years old walking home from school alone, and I see something hanging on the barbed wire of the fence. It's an eagle. A dead eagle. People do that. Hang dead things on fences. Wedge-tailed eagles, foxes, snakes. Things they've killed. And next to the eagle is something else. A piece of rag caught on the wire. No, that's not right. I don't understand. On the barbed wire, are the underpants of a little girl. They are pink, just like Tania's.

———— CHAPTER SEVEN ————

Tarquin and Lucretia

A letter arrives in the mail from the solicitors acting for my brothers. The land still needs to be officially valued, but the blocks I asked for will be transferred to me. Brendan and Mickey are selling the farmhouse and their land so I have to leave. To make a home, I must start again. Like Sarah. But what is home? It's not my old bedroom with its cold fireplace and green Jesus on his cross, shining in the night like uranium. Or the sitting room with the Immaculate Heart of Mary on the mantelpiece with her tilted head and sad eyes. This house does not belong to me.

So, is home Tower Court, with the autumn light falling across the street in blocks of blunt gold? Coffee mornings with Hillary on North Terrace at Il Vero Café? Looking at my shoes as I hurry through the fallen drifts of plane tree leaves on my way to catch the train, the branches above me stiff and bare? Or is home this hill above the Ippinitchie in an old abandoned garden of broken stone and a she-oak tree? Where my great-grandmother raised her children on home-grown cabbages, milk and prayer. And where you can see the mountains like a smear of blue dust singing into the air, so blue you might think them a painting of a wave.

Has the light from these hills ever reached me? What would happen to me if I let it in?

I want the emptiness at the end of a storm, when the past has been thundered out of the air. I open doors. The cool wind from the south unfurls in the house. The still old air, sour with memory and disappointment, resists. I cleanse the house. I ring Mum's old cowbell in the corners, shaking the old ghosts heavy with dust from their sleeping. The spectral dust rises in eddies from the floor and is blown towards the door by the breeze. I hold my breath so it can't get inside me. But maybe it's too late. Maybe it's already inside whether I want it there or not.

I remember Dad in this room with Brendan and Mickey, a few days after Mum died. I was in my bedroom, but I heard them. Dad said things would have to be done differently now Mum was gone. He said Brendan would have to bring in the cow every night and milk her. And Mickey would have to get the wood in and light the fire. Mickey groaned and Dad whipped him across the ear, a blow so hard I heard Mickey crash to the floor. I imagined his pain echoing in red circles, burning again and again through his face. Just like a Chinese burn. My fingers trembled. I wrapped them around each other to make them stop. I felt a strange sweetness in my mouth. The sweetness of wanting him to hurt.

I dream Mickey is sitting on the miner's couch on the verandah. I watch him from the orange tree where I am digging up the body of a dead bird. He is in his mid thirties, the age he is now. I'm about seven. I know this because the trowel I'm using is very big and my hands are very small. I'm sitting on the ground pretending I am invisible. I look at him through the hole in the handle of the trowel. And I see it, the tear being born from his left eye. Now I'm on the miner's couch, adult sized. Suddenly, we turn quietly and comfortably to stone. Feathers rise up out of the ground. I step out of my stone body and float away with them. I look back. He is still there. Still stone.

The rain comes in the night and wakes me. Its sound is heavy on the iron roof like the noise of five thousand galahs passing overhead. A cloud of birds that does not seem to end. I imagine water running down the mountains where a million rivulets combine in nameless streams with lifetimes of less than an hour. They converge again and again until they become a single wave thundering down the channel of the river over the quiet pools, the roots of the red gums and the tendrils of the reeds. I remember the sound was like a train.

Dad would say, 'Can you kids hear that? That's the Ippinitchie coming down.'

———

Betty Crighton is sitting on the verandah in a wheelchair, with a crocheted rug across her knees and a red scarf around her head. The skin on her face looks like wax.

I offer to make us tea. Her kitchen is still green. Along the top of the stained glass cabinet is the same line of vases in green Depression glass that I remember. Nothing has changed except for the woodstove; there is no old silver kettle steaming on the hob. A microwave oven sits there instead, its green light reminding me of the hour. I make a pot of tea and bring it out on a tray.

'The farm looks good,' I say.

'Agnes is doing a fine job of it. She's up on the tractor in the high paddock spraying.'

'Agnes on a tractor?'

'I thought she'd be a teacher, but "no", she said. She wants to farm. Well, with no sons in the family, I could hardly say no. So off she went to agricultural college.'

'She must have done well there?'

'Oh yes, she did. And that's where she met Anthony. Now they work the farm together. It took me a while to come around to the idea of the two of them living here together. It wouldn't have happened in my time, but the farm has never looked better.' Betty leans forward and takes my hand. 'I'm so glad you've come. So very glad.' She pauses and says, 'When you telephoned and said you wanted to come and see me I was thrilled, just thrilled. Look at you. I can't believe the little girl with the blue ribbons in her hair is you. Your mother would be so proud.'

'I hope so.'

'I was sorry to hear about Jack.'

'Thank you. It feels like the end of an era.'

I press my finger against the lid of the china teapot as I pour. The gold strainer turns dark with leaves.

Betty says, 'A lot of the old characters have gone now. Poor old Hopper Quinn, Aunty Nell, now your Dad.'

'And even Cousin Teddie, two years ago this Christmas,' I say.

Betty leans towards the table and stirs her tea. 'So are you going to tell me?' she asks.

'Tell you what?'

'It's all right. I may not have lived in the city like you, but I've worked with people all my life. I know when someone has something on their mind. And you are one of those someones.'

'You've taken me by surprise.'

Betty laughs, 'It's no good getting old if you don't get cunning.'

'Are you well enough to talk? I mean I don't want to—'

'Cassie, it's not your job to protect me. I can look after myself. I've done it all my life. I'm not going to stop now just because I have cancer.'

'Yes, yes, I'm sorry. I'm just not certain how to begin, but I do want to ask you about something that happened a long time ago.'

'I'm old. Everything happened a long time ago to me.' Betty looks at me. 'It's got something to do with Tania Pepper, hasn't it?'

'Why do you say that?'

'The moment I saw Kristyn, I knew she was related to Tania. I thought at first maybe her cousin. When I heard her laugh I thought she might even be a sister. Even after all these years I will never forget Tania's laugh.'

'Kristyn told me she never heard Tania laugh. Not once.'

'It makes me so very sad to hear you say that.'

'Do you know what happened to her?'

'I put two and two together. Whether it's time to say anything about it ... well, that's another matter altogether. But they've all gone now. All the people who could be upset by it. They had their lives in peace.'

I want to ask what that means, but decide not to interrupt. I think of Tania's road and the peace she never found.

Betty says, 'When I first saw Tania, I wanted to sign the papers then and there. I didn't know anything about her family situation, but I was more than happy to take her on. And things were going well, though Beverly was terribly rough on her. Cruel isn't putting too fine a point on it. She was jealous, but I tried to keep things in perspective. I knew given time, Beverly would come around.'

'Do you know what happened the day Tania disappeared?'

'Disappeared? She didn't disappear.'

'I thought she ran away.'

'Goodness no,' she says. She picks up her cup of tea from the side table next to her chair. 'It's strange, isn't it? Just when I think it will all die with me, here you are.'

'Yes.'

She looks at me closely as if she's searching for a way in. She says, 'You were so little when Clare died.'

'I was seven.'

'Too young.'

'I was lucky though, I had Aunty Nell.'

'Yes, yes you did. Nell was one of a kind.' She places her cup and saucer back on the table. She suddenly coughs. The sound is deep and sour. 'Cassie, I'll tell you what I can. But what you do with it after that, as far as Kristyn goes, well that's up to you. I've never said anything to Kristyn. She's too professional to ask and, well, I didn't want to go raising all that sorrow with her if there was no need.'

'I understand,' I say.

'I will never forget the day. It was May 22, 1967, the week we had to vote. I was at the clothesline bringing in the washing, so that's how I know it was the Monday. I was pulling down the sheets from the line. Poor Agnes, always wetting the bed. I used up every sheet in the house, every week for a year. So that's how I came to see Tania coming down the paddock. My first thought was the time. Was it that late already that the kiddies were out of school? When I looked up again, I could see she was in the cattle trough. Her clothes were thrown on the ground. I thought to myself, "What does that girl think she's up to?" I went over to give her a good talking to.

'When I got up close, she was in a dreadful state. Howling and waving her arms around. I said to her, "Dear God child, what on earth has happened?" I tried to lift her out of the trough. But she wouldn't have a bar of it. There was slime from the trough all over her. In her hair, her mouth ... a dreadful state. I picked up her clothes. There was blood on her pinafore. I knew. I knew what had happened. I knew.

'I asked her to give me her hand and told her I'd look after her. I don't know how many times I said it, but finally she reached up for me. I took her in my arms. I checked her over for broken bones. I couldn't find any, but I could see the bruises and swellings on her legs and her wrists.'

'Oh god, she was raped, wasn't she? That's why she was in the trough. The water.'

'I carried her up to the house and put her on my bed. Then I ran her a bath. I stayed with her all night. I didn't leave her. Not for a minute. The next morning, the Tuesday, I telephoned John Henry at the schoolhouse and told him that Tania would not be coming back to school. I said she'd got herself into a spot of trouble and it would be better all 'round for the kiddies if he just carried on as if she'd never been there. For the next two days, I stayed with her. Not for a minute did I leave her. Then on the Thursday morning, I telephoned the services in Adelaide. I didn't dare take the train in case someone saw us. So while the kiddies were at school, I got into the car and drove her to Adelaide. On the way home, I said to myself that it was the best for everyone concerned if I just got on with it, as if nothing had ever happened.

'I never heard from her again. Oh, I made enquiries, but they assured me she was being taken care of. I didn't know what else to do. I had three kiddies of my own to look after and she was in such a terrible state. I said to the girls that Tania's real parents wanted her back and they were never to mention her name again.'

'Did you tell the police?'

'How could I? I would have been blamed.'

'For what had happened?'

'No, for telling the truth. You were only young, Cassie. It was different then. You mark my words, in the time around that '67 referendum – well, some people were uncertain about what to think. But I could just imagine what a lot of them would have said if I'd spoken up: *Fancy ruining local families over what had happened to an Aborigine.* That's what they would have thought. Before that referendum, the Aborigines weren't even included in the census, but there were some people around here, they didn't say it out loud, but I know they voted against it.'

'Tania didn't count, did she? She literally didn't count.'

'She counted to me, but what could I do?'

'What about justice? She deserved that, didn't she?'

'I'm sorry I couldn't give it to her.'

'Did she tell you who it was?'

'I knew. But if I'd said anything, lives would have been left in ruins. Innocent lives. I couldn't live with that on my conscience. So I didn't say a word. And besides, what would have become of *her*? She didn't have tuppence to her name. Not even a bank account. Everything came from him. In those days, the husbands left everything to the son. Never the poor wife. But when Rex and I were first engaged, I said everything was to be in both our names, or I wouldn't marry him.

'You know Cassie, I nearly told the police at first, but then on the

Thursday morning, Moira phoned me with the news about your mother. Oh, such terrible news. The whole district was in shock at losing Clare. But I knew then what I had to do about Tania and that was that.'

'I don't understand. What's Mum's death got to do with any of this?'

'Do you really want to know, Cassie? Once I tell you, there's no going back. I wanted everyone to live out their lives without the burden of it all. And that includes you.'

'I have to know. I need the truth.'

'Oh, Cassie. Nell. Your Aunty Nell. It would have broken her. And then what would have happened to you and the boys if she wasn't there all those years looking after you?'

'I don't understand.'

'It was Teddie. Your cousin Teddie.'

'No, that's not right. That can't be right.' He wasn't like that. He wasn't. He is my blood. The grandson of Sarah. The son of Aunty Nell. My blood. My poor beloved Irish blood. My chest burns with anger. I say, 'Tania told you that?'

The spoon rattles sharply against her cup. 'Yes, she did. And I believed her. But the truth is no one else would have.'

All my life I have wanted the truth. And now I have it. The truth to set me free. It strikes like a lightning bolt that sends me falling from my tower. Because I believe her too.

Betty says, 'It went round and round in my head about what to do. But I knew Tania would have been traumatised all over again if I went to the police, and for what? For nothing.'

There is silence. She waits for me to speak. 'But what if you'd stood up for her?'

'Ah, yes,' Betty says. 'For years, I thought, what if someone asks me that very question? How would I answer? Well, this is my answer. I had my girls to think of Cassie. My girls.'

My anger sharpens. 'Yes, and all those committees, all that respect you have around here would have vanished, wouldn't it? If you stood by an Aboriginal girl against your own neighbours.'

She leans forward and looks at me sternly. Her eyes are warm and shining. She does not blink. 'I had obligations, Cassie. Responsibilities. To the district.'

I stop the car and get out near the school. I can see the old apricot tree at the edge of the playground. The gum trees are different shapes now. I don't recognise them. The road is rich in shadow from new saplings. I walk along the fence. It is new cyclone with silver-grey barbed wire. I look for the old rocks I remember. Anything that is familiar. But the things that once gave me my coordinates have gone: the red gum with the dead limb, the yellow chunk of sandstone that rested for years on the side of the road. The wild stand of dog rose. All gone. So what is still here?

I reach the old footbridge over the Ippinitchie. It is broken now. Long grey slabs of timber hang down against the riverbank. The river flows slowly by. I remember I was running when I reached the bridge that day, so I've come too far. I decide to run back along the road towards the school hoping my body will remember the distance. I stop about two hundred and fifty metres from the bridge.

I pick up a stick and walk slowly along the road, not looking for markers anymore but for guidance. I breathe. I know the memory is in me.

I say out loud, 'Show me where to stop.'

The stick drags in the dirt. I am six years old and my sandals are filling with grit. I am thinking about Tania Pepper in the apricot tree, how she kissed me on the cheek. How I gave her half a scone. How she wanted to go home.

A shudder in my body makes me stop.

I look up at the fence. Nothing is the same. But I know it was here. The wire is as tight as a wall. I cannot bend it to climb through. I find the nearest post, place my foot in the cyclone and climb over.

The paddock is a thin scrub of dog wattle and blue gums. I'm looking for a place. A place with a purpose. In a broken sheath of bark by my foot, a beetle with a rainbow on its back clambers by a star of white web. In front of me, the red rumps of the grass parrots shine like kites as they weave over the rocks and around the Christmas bushes.

I walk through a stand of wattles and into a row of ancient red gums that follow the curved line of the Ippinitchie. I listen to the wind and the crush of leaves under my shoes. I feel waves tumbling across me, then through me.

I hurry now to the last of the red gums before the river bends eastward through a floodgate. The base of the tree is rounded as if the trunk were made of swollen muscle, distended from centuries of holding on to the earth. I step over the sheddings of its bark towards the cavern of the tree. The opening is thick with orb webs. I use my stick to brush them away. They crackle and stretch but do not break. Inside, the tree is black, crosshatched with fractal lines. I fall to my knees and start to push away the leaves on the ground with my hands. In the corner, I find what I am looking for. This object of history. Her history and mine. A skipping rope with red handles.

I lie on the sitting room floor with my arms curled around my chest as if I'm cold. As if my bones are filled with hail.

My Irish blood. You know what it is to suffer at the hands of tyranny.

So tell me this: how could you still have so much cruelty left in you?

My body kicks and shakes. I growl in rings, low and deep. Now, howls, sharp-edged and high. My noise. My howls. This is all I hear for a long time. Because every time I close my eyes this is what I see: close up his hair is the size of trees, his arms are the size of a mountain range.

I sit on the miner's couch on the verandah with the skipping rope at my feet.

What can I do? Who can I tell?

Over and over, I imagine taking Dad's gun, and shooting Teddie through the heart. Over and over, I watch him die. But he is safe. Forever. And unreachable. Death does that.

Stars are reflected in the kitchen window as if suspended there in black glass. The moon has not yet risen. I find some brown paper from Dad's kitchen drawer. I wrap the skipping rope, and put it on the hot water heater by the windowsill. Outside.

The pain chisels at Kristyn's face. The quiet tears fall. She listens until the end. Later she says, 'I've nursed some. Young. Helped them through the examination. Written down the wounds. The ones that can be written down ... I never heard her laugh. Not once. You said you can still remember her laugh. Tell me again. What was it like?'

'It lives in you. Betty said that's how she recognised you. She thought you were Tania's sister, because your laugh is exactly like hers.'

'There was no justice for Tania, was there?'

'No, none. All you have is the truth. And that's nowhere near enough.'

She says, 'I told you once that Tania was hooked on the deadliest poison there is. She said to me when things were bad, "When I close my eyes, I don't want to see what I see. I just want to see nothing. The peace and black of nothingness". I didn't know what she meant, but I do now. Every time she closed her eyes, she saw him.' She turns to me and says, 'How could she possibly live with that?'

I woke up this morning dreaming about Titian's *Tarquin and Lucretia*. Titian was in his eighties when he created this painting in 1570. Lucretia, a Roman wife, is naked on a bed of white pillows, her face flushed with terror. Above her, holding a knife, is Tarquin, the last prince of Rome. He is dressed in red. His right knee is thrust between her thighs. Lucretia's servant girl looks on in horror. What is not in the painting is what follows. Lucretia tells her family of the rape and says she cannot live with the dishonour and then takes her own life. The men of the city rise up against Tarquin and cast him out. But why is she the one to die?

The sky is low today with stratus cloud, shapeless and grey. The ranges have disappeared in a long wave of settled mist. We are sitting in the garden next to a little fire of fallen grey box and kindling from the orange trees. The smoke rises in the windless air.

Kristyn asks, 'What would you have done if you were Betty?'

I wait for an answer to come. Eventually, I say, 'Told the truth. Stood up for Tania. I know Betty thinks that would have left Aunty Nell with no one, but she could have lived with us. And if not us, someone else would have taken her in. There are good people around here. When Mrs Piper's husband was killed in 1961, the local baker, Mr Fidget, gave her a free loaf of bread every day for the rest of her life.' A breeze appears and turns the smoke of the fire towards my eyes. I try to wave it away. I say, 'But I can't judge Betty on the choice she made. All I can say is if I had been in her shoes, I hope I would have done it differently. Though it's easy for me to say that. I have the benefits of a very different culture.'

Her voice smarts with irritation, 'You were brought up with the same culture as she was. Can't you see that?'

'Betty was born in the 1920s.'

'You're missing the point. The culture I'm talking about says if Tania had been a white girl, Betty would have contacted the police.'

I look to the ashes at the edge of the fire, 'I don't know that.'

'Yes, you do, but you don't want to see it. Even you. Tania didn't count. She didn't count, because she was black.'

'You can't blame Betty. She was a product of her time.'

'It was Betty's responsibility to look after her regardless of what fucking century she was in. She didn't. What happened to Tania didn't matter as much as if it'd happened to a white girl and that's the truth.'

'Men brutalise women and girls regardless of what race they are.'

'He chose her because she was black.'

'You don't know that. Maybe he chose her because she was a girl.'

Kristyn leans towards me.

'Okay, well answer this. Did you ask Betty why she wasn't worried about the safety of her own daughters by letting him go free? And what about your safety? Christ, you used to pass his house walking home from school. Why wasn't she worried about you? Did you ask her that?'

'No, I didn't.'

'Why didn't you, Cassandra? Why didn't you ask her?'

'I don't know.'

'Because you and Betty both know, so it goes without saying, doesn't it? You were never in danger from him. Neither were her daughters. And you were never in danger for one reason. Because you're white.'

At my feet, the hot coals of the fire darken. I pick up a branch and turn them back towards the flame. I hold the branch too tightly. It hurts my fingers, but that is the only way I can stop my hands from shaking. The smoke burns my eyes.

I say, 'So where does this leave you ... nursing Betty?'

'It doesn't make any difference. I'll look after her. It's my job.' She looks at me sharp-eyed and says, 'It's my responsibility.'

The light seeps under the blind and spreads outwards like a rising tide.

Kristyn phones and says, 'Where's her skipping rope?'

'I didn't know what to do with it, so I wrapped it up. It's on the hot water service by the kitchen window.'

'I'd like to have it. Leave it there, and I'll pick it up tonight. I think it's been outside long enough.'

So this is the geology of tears: I lie on the floor alone in the house, my arms outstretched on the lino, my body breaking open along its fault lines. Waves of sorrow shake me and tears flood into my ears. One word rolls around the room, crashing against the walls and into the corners of my brain. Over and over. *Scotoma*.

I am searching for the past. My past. My culture. I go to my mother's cupboard and pull out her Catholic prayer books. I read the *Commentary on the Catechism*. A clergyman of the Catholic Church, responsible for explaining the principles of the faith to millions, wrote this line in 1949, just eleven years before I was born:

The Australian Aborigines are considered to be physically and mentally one of the lowest types of race.

My autograph book is in the back of my wardrobe under a white cosmetic case and a plastic bag full of old Christmas cards. The cover of the book is worn smooth and there is a ruffle of torn paper where the first page used to be. I remember Mickey drew a picture of me on that page with my fingers up my nose. Inside, each page is pastel. Pink. Yellow. Green. Muted blues. Professor O'Grady used to say, 'Pastels have a faint heart. They are colours that are ashamed of themselves. Or should be.' I flick through the pages. They are pale as if they were fugitive colours, injured by light and time.

Towards the back I read:

> *God made the little niggers*
> *He made them in the night*
> *He made them in a hurry*
> *And forgot to paint them white.*

The autograph is Moira McKenzie's. I throw the book into the rubbish bin. I get it out again from under two dripping milk cartons. I step outside and burn it with the milk cartons and a newspaper. The ash spreads along the ground and into the air. It's gone now. But it was there. It was.

Each life does harm. We know this to be true. That's why people need God. To forgive the unforgiveable.

I know the names from an ocean away. Apache. And Comanche. Cheyenne and Sioux. The great Native American nations. I know the names of warriors who fought the invaders. Geronimo. Sitting Bull. Cochise. Crazy Horse. I even know the name of a battle. Little Bighorn. And I know the name of the man who led the government troops into that battle. George Custer. I also know he died there.

But in my country we were taught there were no Aboriginal nations who owned their land. No Aboriginal warriors who fought the invaders. No battles. The land was settled. Not stolen. Because the land was the land of nobody. *Terra nullius*. Today the High Court of Australia says what we were taught was a lie. I hear the news on the radio. It is 3 June 1992. The day I learn a new word. A name. *Mabo*.

My words come slowly to Kristyn over the phone.

'I'm so sorry. I didn't mean to hurt you.'

'You didn't. You just showed me you've got no idea what it's like to be black.'

'Well, you'd better come over so you can tell me then ... what it's like ...'

'Is that why you want to see me?' Her voice rises with anger. 'So I can help you work out how your thinking is racist?'

'That's not what I mean ... I want to listen to whatever you have to say ... about anything.'

Kristyn suddenly laughs, 'You've missed me.'

———

One night in the shapeless dark, after the moon has set, Kristyn says, 'I'm lost, Cassandra.'

I want to tell her she can't be lost, because I know where she is. Her head is against my shoulder. She is here with me at Ippinitchie River, Southern Flinders Ranges, South Australia. This is the latitude and the longitude of her. Of us.

'Eddie Mabo knew where he belonged. He was a Meriam man. I want to belong somewhere.' She turns towards me. I can tell this even in the dark, because I feel her breath glow against my throat. 'I had a message today from a woman I've been trying to track down. She's been overseas, but now she's back in Melbourne. She said she knows someone who can tell me something about my mother.'

Her body is now in eclipse. The light at the rim of her is so bright it hurts my eyes.

'And I suppose palliative care in Melbourne is always looking for nurses.'

'Yes.'

'When will you leave?'

'When Betty dies.'

I say, 'I will imagine white light around her then, every day healing her.'

Her hand reaches for mine. She holds it to her cheek where she knows I can feel her tears.

'So will I.'

The cancer spreads like poison into the worn-out lungs of Betty Crighton. Agnes holds her while she dies.

The Church of England is already full by the time I arrive for her funeral. I stand outside with hundreds of people while the songs and eulogies and final farewells to Elizabeth Anne (Betty) Crighton are broadcast to us through an amplifier. I am here today because the dark matter in the universe of my heart wants Beverly to see me. So my presence can remind her to feel something about Tania. Regret or shame. When she steps out of the church I see her. Not all at once. In the spaces between the black-suited shoulders and hats of the people of Ippinitchie River I see fragments of her. As if she were a painting by Picasso. A cheekbone. A curl of hair. The curved brim of her fedora.

I want the people here to see the child that I remember. Monstrous. Cruel. But they shake her hand. They hold her. And now what I see makes me turn away and walk back to my car: the three Crighton sisters are standing together as the coffin carrying their mother is lifted into the hearse. Their arms are wrapped around each other. Beverly is in the middle with her hand open on the small of Agnes's back. I see the tension in her fingers. As if she were holding her up. Scaffolding strong enough to stop Agnes from falling.

———————

Kristyn is out walking. Sarah's Garden. The Ippinitchie. Other places. She may not know why she's out there, but I know. She is doing this so all of her can leave. She is out there gathering up any pieces of her soul that during her time here have sloughed off against the rocks, or have fallen to the ground without her noticing. Perhaps she might be leaving things behind as well. Like memory. But I don't know if it's possible to do that. This is the last night. I know when I wake tomorrow Kristyn will not be here. And this room will be a hollow like the inside of a bell that may never ring out again with the music of her.

Before I open my eyes I know. I hear the absence of her as if it were a voice calling out from every room in the house: *She's gone. She's gone. She's gone.*

I hear the magpies outside piping on the grass. Today is the first day of September, but the house is winter cold. I pull up the blinds and the sunlight rushes in, bursting against the yellow walls of the kitchen. Resting against the coffeepot on the table is an envelope with *Cassandra* written in black cursive. Why has she done this when we'd promised no sad last words? I make myself a coffee and take it outside to the verandah. Above me is the first blue of the flowers on the wisteria vine. I open the envelope. Inside is a little package. Filled with seeds of the she-oak.

———

In the night silence, I hear her breath. I feel the curve of her body pressed against me, but it's not her. It's just the tender weight of the sheet folded against my skin.

> *And when they ask me why the tears, I'll say*
> *'I miss your remembering of me'.*

Today, I plant seven she-oak seedlings along the ridge at Sarah's Garden from the seeds Kristyn gave to me. I found my path to her through my own soul. Is that how I find a road home? Through my own soul?

Early September shifts the air, pulls at the buds until they burst, humming with bees. Along the river, the fronds of the sedges crack as I walk by, and millions of tiny insects shine like flecks of dust in the thick afternoon air. From the ground to the wattles to the shining tops of the river reds, the country throbs and pulses as if it were a wire singing in the wind.

I say into the phone, 'Professor O'Grady, is that you? ... Can you help me? I can't find my way into the canvas.'

'To be an artist, you need great courage, Cassandra. You have to press your open eyes into whatever separates you from the truth, especially the truth you fear the most.'

What truth do I fear? I don't know. Or do I lack the courage to ask?

—— CHAPTER EIGHT ——

An Old Bee Farm

I clean up the farmhouse. Four generations of my family. There is less here than I have accumulated so far in my lifetime. But what do you keep from the past? What do you let go? In a cardboard box, I pack *The Schoolgirls' Bumper Book*, the photograph of the war memorial unveiling at Ippinitchie River, and my drawing of Tania. I hold it up to the light. I kiss her on the cheek.

Col's sister runs an antique store in Laura. Two men arrive in a green truck, and three hours later the house is empty. In these rooms, my footsteps sound so loud, but soon I'll be back in the noise of the city. I won't hear them there.

Objects can hold so much sorrow. I open the wooden box that contains my mother's rosary and feel it release its scents of grief. They remind me of the rich fragrances of the dampness under stones, where the centipedes and lizards shelter and the spiders draw their nests of silver. The coordinates of my mother's life: blood, geography and time, in a broken circle of wooden beads that has counted a million prayers.

My father is buried in the Ippinitchie Cemetery next to my

mother where a line of radiata pines sends the afternoon sun into heavy shadow. His headstone says, *Beloved husband of Clare, beloved father of Brendan, Michael and Cassandra.* The headstone is a thick and heavy grey. It reminds me of a book. But not one that is loved. One that is feared. One that contains laws, codes. Expectations.

I say a long goodbye to my mother. When I get back to the city, I will wind up her mantel clock so it can chime out once more the passing hours of my life.

Aunty Nell is buried in the row west of my parents. I don't know why it has taken me all this time to read the letter she wrote to me so long ago:

Dear Cassie,

Don't be too surprised at getting a letter from me. I know you're all grown up now with a life of your own and that's the way it should be. The nurses here are very kind. The Auxiliary ladies come every Tuesday afternoon as noisy as a bunch of fowls. They help the old dears with their greeting cards or just sit and have a cup of tea with them. Betty Crighton has taught me how to do lace making. It gives me something to do of a night. I don't remember a lot of what I should, being in my eighties now, but what I do remember is you on the old verandah drawing the geraniums. I've forgotten most of the things now on account of my mind isn't what it was. But what I do remember is you were sunshine.

Love from

Aunty Nell

I say out loud to the air and the ground, 'I'm so sorry Aunty Nell I never said thank you for teaching me to read, for teaching me how to see the light of things, for looking after me all those years. That you died without ever hearing me say those things.' From my pocket, I take a little glass jar filled with earth that I gathered from Sarah's Garden high above the river, where once a woodstove burned and a table was set. From there, it feels as though you can see through time. I empty the earth across her grave.

I go to Sarah's Garden for comfort. The labours of my great-grandmother fall back to earth. Here is the shape of a post hollowed out of the stone, the space where the crossbeams once held up the roof. The mortar of dirt and water still holds on, a rich and rufous brown the colour of a kestrel wing. There is little wood left here now. The dark trails of the white ants have fed on my family's past. An old hardwood post, silver-grey and lined with dark seams, is turned on its side. One day it will fall to dust. Already, a crack runs down and across its furrows, the waves of age and sun. At my feet, the kangaroo and spear grasses rise up between the stones.

I look around to the rocks, the grass, the she-oak. I do not say the words, but I feel such thankfulness. I remember Kristyn here. The first sight of her on my bed of she-oak leaves and grass. The firelight falling off her breasts and thighs. She was so beautiful, like dark earth, I could hardly speak. Whenever I touched her, at the end of my fingertips was the light of flowers.

I look out across the farm and I say to the stones, the trees and the faces of the hills, 'I came here with a broken heart and you have sheltered me.'

The late afternoon sun shows us the folds and curves of the world. Shapes we cannot see in the rest of the day. They rise as the light and shadows fall into them. I am looking now at a single stone at Sarah's Garden. It has some sort of fault line, a bruise from years of winters and sun. My body weeps now, because I recognise it. I have found the keystone from Sarah's fireplace that Aunty Nell told me about so long ago. *Sarah, you were here.* If it hadn't been for the afternoon sun, I would never have seen it. Four spokes shaped like sheaves meet in a square. I know what it is. The Cross of Saint Brigid you carved into the stone.

———————

The chorography of a river.

The headlands of the Ippinitchie are where the mountains rise out of their birth-lines and the run-off gathers in the folds of the tilted earth. The water descends onwards to the sea, past the shale and scree of the hills until, by a sandstone reef, it slips back into its silky shadows in the ground, filling the deep springs. And where the river reeds and sedges grow, water trickles out of the rock. Until the coming of the blue autumn rain, this is where the frogs grow and the euro bends to drink, dampening her soft jaws.

I remember long ago climbing over the fence of the house paddock, rolling the blue ribbons and rubber bands out of my plaits, and running down to the river. When running felt like flying and I glided over the thistle and the stone.

I remember the timbre of this river. How I could put my hands to my chest, and the tremolo there from my heart was the same rhythm as the flowing water.

I remember in summer looking up at the dry cliffs of the river and seeing how the roots and the earth and stones enfolded each other.

I remember the last of the river pools darkened by fallen leaves and stillness. That stillness was a home for me no one could touch or open.

Soon, more rain will come and the rhythm of the Ippinitchie will flow again through the air and past the sedges along the riverbanks. And the blue gum flowers will scatter across the ground as if the shadows of every tree were made of sunlight.

I want to be here to see it. And to watch the streaks of foam slip over the stones like the freezing breath of winter, and the light floating on the river as if it were made of pages of gold, dissolving over and over beneath the water.

Cousin Tom will lend me his caravan until my house is finished at Sarah's Garden. I phone Hillary to tell her my plans.

'God,' she says, 'you're re-building from a ruin? On a hill at the back end of nowhere?'

I say, 'I'm going to be like the woman in Clara Southern's painting, *An Old Bee Farm*. On my own in the bush.'

'Christ, darling, what will you do for sex? I will visit you often and bring along suitable company to keep you young.'

———

A man on TV wears a hat made out of a feral cat. Some people hate him for doing it. Some love him. He says words I've never heard. *Dunnart, bilby, bettong* and *quoll*. He says they are the animals that once called the Southern Flinders home. They are gone now. Not moved on to somewhere else. Not disappeared. The colonists destroyed their bushland homes and now the animals are dead. Turned to dust.

I climb the hill and look along the silver lines of the fences. I think how every paddock was once a forest. And how every forest paid for my family and me. And so did the cattle and the sheep taken away to Mr Cobb's slaughterhouse on the hill above the town. They paid for everything I ever had. Every meal. Every dress and every toy.

The magpies and the swallows see me and fly away. The euros turn their heavy shoulders from me and bound into the shelter of the trees, watching me carefully from the shadows. Have we made our country afraid of the sound of our footsteps on the grass? I remember the grey box trees when Dad was driving us home at night. When the headlights touched them, they appeared out of the dark full and white like ghosts. Were they just like a kangaroo on the night road, shocked and frozen by the impossible glare of us? Does the country remember what we have done? Perhaps we are not the only ones on earth who tell stories to one another.

I am here now and so I must begin. I want to see with an artist's eyes. Can I be that brave? Whenever I look at the truth of my world, my eyes hurt. But every day, I will walk this land to see what I can see. I need to know this country as if it were the body of my child.

Across the eastern slope of the hill, the light thickens with dust where the grass and stubble are chewed down to the quick. Parts of the hillside are scarred where the topsoil is sliding away towards the Ippinitchie. The rich ranges' loam that feeds the crops that feed the world is slipping down the river to the gulf waters of the sea. Cattle hooves have dug holes in the banks of the river. The sedges lie broken. And the pools are silent. No calling of the frogs. No tadpoles in the water. And when I look into the trees, I see no frogmouths shape-shifting into broken wood. They have disappeared without me even noticing. I don't know why they have gone or what I can do to bring them back.

I know so little. What is being spoken one to the other? The blue bee to the red gum, the red gum to the river, the river to the sedges and the stone? What does the owl need to feed her children? Why do the ants change the colour of the stones upon their nests? What do the choughs say when they call to each other across the high trees?

I learn the names of the bushland plants from *Wildflowers of the Southern Flinders Ranges*. Old Man's Beard. Eggs and Bacon. Running Postman. I look for where they grow. I learn the anatomy of she-oaks. The long tendrils of the she-oak that move and cry in the wind are not leaves. They are branchlets. And along each one, evenly spaced in whorls, are the tiny leaves. The she-oak breathes through circles of gold.

The circuitry of the dictator is burnt into my brain: I can take what I want. I can kill for my desire. I want to poison the kangaroo grass to plant roses and a lawn.

———

I need to see the sea.

I go to Port Germein into the blue body of the ranges, past the forests of grass trees on the northern slopes and the sheer rock walls of sandstone and quartzite stretching high into the air all around me. In 1951, Dorrit Black came here to paint landscapes of this gorge with the contrasting colours of orange and green. *Rock Face* and *Landslide* both subtitled *at Port Germein Gorge*. Professor O'Grady had said, 'Dorrit Black reminds us that while she travelled and worked in Europe, she knew just as Hans Heysen did, the art in the South Australian landscape is right before us waiting for our brushes and our hearts'.

The sea in the rich afternoon light is the colour of a she-oak in flower. I walk the jetty at Port Germein over the incoming tide that stretches as shallows for more than one and a half kilometres. Under my feet the jetty supports are a hundred years old, the giant eucalypts of the Southern Flinders forests. At the end of the jetty, I lean against the railing to watch the waves come in. Floating on the water nearby is a scattering of red petals. I wonder where they have come from. Perhaps they are the vestiges of a wedding or a birthday. Or flowers taken in a storm from someone's garden. Each wave carries the memory of the wind.

I lean over the edge of the jetty listening to the sound of the waves and watching the petals until they are carried into the shadows beneath me. I am thinking about the colour red. The colour of Christmas. Fire. Blood. Rage and love. In 1621 Guercino used it beautifully in his painting *Christ and the Woman Taken in Adultery*. It is the story from the Gospel of St John, the moment when Christ says to the men who want to kill her, 'He that is without sin among you, let him cast the first stone'. Christ and the accused woman are wearing the same colour red. Matisse knew about the power of red, so did Vincent van Gogh and the impressionists. And once I must have known it too.

As I turn to go, I think how so many paintings I have come to know use the power of red. Most I have loved. But there are also some I never want to contemplate again. *Ajax and Cassandra*. And the one I saw hanging in the landing in the home of Molly and Keith Schurmann. The one called *Sarah's Garden*. The painting that was meant to investigate the relationships between European settlement and country, entropy and time. But it did something more. It stopped me painting. It stopped me. It is without red, apart from the blossom of a single geranium flower encircled by barbed wire. I remember what Professor O'Grady said to me, 'To be an artist, you need great courage, Cassandra. You have to press your open eyes into whatever separates you from the truth, especially the truth you fear the most.' I was named after the prophet Cassandra. But I can't see into the future. Only the past.

I am seven years old walking home alone from school. I don't know it yet, but in two days my mother will die. As I look ahead past the line of acacias and blue gum saplings, I see a dead wedge-tailed eagle on the barbed wire fence. Her wings are stretched out like the arms of Jesus on the cross. Next to the dead bird is a pair of pink underpants. I feel frightened and I don't know why. Suddenly, I hear a vehicle come charging along the road. So I do what Mum and Dad have taught me to do. I hide behind a bush until it goes past. It might be a stranger. But the vehicle brakes sharply, skidding to a halt in great clouds of dust, so thick my eyes start to water. The driver's side door opens, and through the dust, I see someone tear the underpants from the wire. It isn't a stranger. She is wearing a printed frock covered in red geranium flowers. It is Aunty Nell.

Through the dark of the moon I go home.

I go back through the open heart of the mountains. I go home to where the shape of the pain is carved into the country, like the motion of water imprinted on stone. These shapes tell us what forces have been here transforming the world: a curve in the riverbank, a hollow in the cliff, or the objects of history, the vestigium of lives now gone. A keystone carved with the Cross of Saint Brigid. The waves of a war never named in a skipping rope with red handles.

———

I am learning to enter slowly into the bushland at Sarah's Garden. I sit on a stone and wait until I feel the air open, the grass soften, and the magpie return to her branch. She sings to me now just a few steps from my shoulder. I see the body of a dead skink by the she-oak tree. The atoms of its eyes are already in my lungs. The wattle seed crushed beneath my feet has already worked its way into my body. Pressed into my right toe, and in the blood flowing through my heart. I cancel my order for lawn seed at Ippinitchie Service-Mart. I let my roses die. The kangaroo grass will grow to my door.

I am looking at an artist's catalogue for the colour blue: Heather Blue. Cornflower Blue. Persian Blue. Prussian Blue. Oxford Blue. Robin's Egg Blue. But these colours, I don't know them. What meaning can the blue of the American robin's egg have in the lands of the Ippinitchie, where the eggs of the flame and scarlet robins are patched with purple, and the hooded robin has eggs of olive green? I need new names for the colour blue: the blue of summer horizons heavy with twilight and dust, the blue of the fairy wren and the eye on a gum moth wing. I need names for the colours of this country: a red for the heath and quandong, and the stems of the eucalyptus after rain, the grey of frogmouth feathers and box tree bark, the crimson softness of galahs, the golds of the kangaroo grass and the she-oak when they flower.

Every week the seven trees I planted along the ridge grow taller. I say a word out loud to each one of them. *Kristyn.* So the sound of her name will sing forever in their leaves.

The box came today in the mail. A carton of brushes and oils, sketch paper and canvas. Charcoal and crayons. I sit on the floor surrounded by the scent of paint. There is still time for the doing of the work. The slow and untidy work of revelation. What remains on the canvas after I have shed everything that is no longer necessary.

Fronds of cloud stretch northward in the sky. Patterns repeat themselves like notes humming together. The rocks along the hilltop are a row of nimbus clouds. Above me, the clouds are the shape of feathers, vertebrae, nebulae, the broken uplifts of rock. The solar system is patterned like an atom. It is made of spheres just like the human face. If I can draw a circle I can draw humanity or the sun. The song of the universe is metaphor reprised over and over. I put my sketchbook on a stone beside me. The low valleys and foothills of the ranges are in a blue shadow. I am watching the unfolding of the blossom of the world.

———

Seven times, I play the message on the answering machine from Kristyn:

'Meet me in Adelaide on the 25th, under the Central Market atrium, and we'll free a few sparrows.'

I map the deserts in her body.

My mouth tastes the stories of her skin.

She lights the sad rivers and valleys around my heart.

'I want to go home,' she says.

———

Today, Kristyn and I are driving north from the city. Tomorrow, we will cross the border into the Territory where she can hear her country's stories in the shimmering light of the red ground, the spinifex and the desert oaks. And with us will be a charcoal drawing. The first drawing I ever did of someone I loved.

Along the highway at Hope View, I see the blue of the Flinders rising out of the plains to the sea. I have never heard the ancient word for these mountains. Perhaps it is a sacred word for the Nukunu and the Adnyamathanha peoples. Perhaps it has been lost in the war. Perhaps there never was just a single name. This blue line of mountains is the birth-line of our country. It is a complicated act for me to look upon that blue and call it home. As we drive by the Southern Flinders a few white clouds appear in the rising air along the hillsides facing the sun. As I let in the light and dark of these mountains, I don't know what will happen to the cartography of my heart. It is late summer, and along the road to Sarah's Garden, the grey box are in flower, the honeyeaters are feeding on the shadowed side of the trees, and the kangaroo grass is shedding its seeds to the wind.

end

Author note

'Catholics, Catholics ring the bell ...' I was taught this song at a family reunion in Adelaide c. 2001 by those who sang it as children in the 1930s on their way to Catholic school. The song was used to taunt any Protestant children they might encounter.

'Fabulous films ...' is my fictional variation of the sentence: 'Finished files are the results of years of scientific study combined with the experience of years.' There are almost two million references on the web to this sentence. I am unable to determine its authorship.

Cassandra's list 'These are the things my mother could do that I can't' was inspired by Timothy O'Grady's 'What I Couldn't Do.' *I Could Read the Sky*. London: The Harvill Press, 1997, p. 71.

My Favourite Martian. 1963–1966. John L. Greene. ABC. Television.

The Schoolgirls' Bumper Book (see below) does not contain any reference to Cassandra and Troy. This is a fiction.

'God made the little niggers ...' as an autograph. c. 1970. Collection of the author. According to *independent.co.uk* (8 December 1996), the rhyme appeared on printed postcards in 1939.

On 17 June 2019, the Federal Court of Australia recognised the Nukunu people as the traditional owners of the lands of the Southern Flinders Ranges.

Glossary

An Gorta Mór 'The Great Hunger'.

Boireann The Burren, 'rocky place'.

Caoine 'the keen'.

Scalpeen 'a temporary rough shelter'.

Tobar Bride 'Brigid's Well'.

Cill Dara 'Kildare'. St Brigid's holy flame burned at the temple here for a thousand years. The keepers of the flame were women.

Poulnabrone Dolmen an ancient portal tomb on the Burren

References

Books

Etiquette: A handbook for all occasions to suit Australian conditions. Northbridge: Certified Productions, 1940, p. 55. Print.

Kroll, Jeri. *Death as Mr Right*. Friendly Street Poets. 1982. Print.

O'Farrell, Patrick. *The Irish in Australia*. (See reference *McCaffrey, the Potato Picker.* below.)

Frean, R.W. *Commentary on the Catechism: A complete course of instruction in the Catholic faith*. Australia: Pellegrini and Co., 1949, p. 40. Print.

Kingsley, Charles. *His Letters, and Memories of His Life*. Vol. 2. 1890. Ed. 'By His Wife' [Frances Eliza Kingsley]. London: Macmillan and Co., 1894. "Visit to Ireland." Chap. XIX. 111-12. *California Digital Library*, University of California, 2008. Web. 20 Dec. 2012. PDF file.

Kingsley, Charles. *The Water-Babies*. 1863. Web.

'Love Is Proved by Suffering.' *The Catholic Religion*. Lesson 15, p. 179. Print.

'My mother said ...' *The Oxford Dictionary of Nursery Rhymes*. Ed. Iona Opie and Peter Opie. Oxford: Oxford University Press, 1980, p. 315. Print.

New Idea. Melbourne: Southdown Press, 11 July 1962. Print.

Pedler, Rosemary. *Wildflowers of the Southern Flinders Ranges*. Plant Identikit. Society for Growing Australian Plants. 1992. Print.

The Schoolgirls' Bumper Book London: Collins (c. 1929) Print.

Sewell, Anna. *Black Beauty*. 1877. Web.

Poetry, Song Lyrics

'Tobar Bride', lyrics by Annette Marner. Music by Anna O'Neil. Used with permission.

'I wish you pain ...', an extract from the poem 'Midnight Drive', Annette Marner, *Women with Their Faces on Fire*, Kent Town: Friendly Street Poets/Wakefield Press, 2006, p. 35. Print.

Paintings, Photographs, Sculptures, Cartoons

Bernini, Gian Lorenzo, *The Ecstasy of St Teresa*. 1647–1652. Marble. Cornaro Chapel, Santa Maria della Vittoria, Rome.

Black, Dorrit, *Rock Face* at Port Germein Gorge. 1951. Private collection. (Reference: Lock-Weir, Tracey. *Dorrit Black Unseen Forces*. Art Gallery of South Australia. Adelaide).

Black, Dorrit, *Landslide* at Port Germein Gorge. 1951. Private collection. (See Lock-Weir as above)

Degas, Edgar. *La Classe de Danse*. Between 1871 and 1874. Oil on canvas. Museé d'Orsay, Paris. *Museé d'Orsay.*

Gentileschi, Artemisia. *Judith Slaying Holofernes*. c. 1613–1614. Oil on canvas. Galleria degli Uffizi, Florence.

Guercino, *Christ and the Woman Taken in Adultery*. c. 1621. Oil on canvas. Dulwich Picture Gallery, London.

'Height of Impudence.' Cartoon. *Punch*, December 1846. *The Irish Famine*. Peter Gray. London: Thames and Hudson, 1995, p. 49. Print.

Matisse, Henri. *La Musique*. 1939. Oil on canvas. Albright-Knox Art Gallery, Buffalo.

Matisse, Henri. *The Sorrows of the King*. 1952. Gouache on papier-découpé. Museé National d'Art, Paris.

McCaffrey, the Potato Picker. 1899. Langham Collection. Ulster Museum, Belfast. O'Farrell. Patrick. *The Irish in Australia.* Rev. edn, Kensington: New South Wales University Press, 1993, p. 61. Print.

McCubbin, Frederick. *The Pioneer.* 1904. Oil on canvas. National Gallery of Victoria, Melbourne.

Solomon, Solomon J. *Ajax and Cassandra.* Oil on canvas. 1886. Art Gallery of Ballarat, Ballarat.

Southern, Clara. *An Old Bee Farm.* c. 1900. Oil on canvas. National Gallery of Victoria, Melbourne.

Sutherland, Jane. *Obstruction, Box Hill.* 1887. Oil on canvas. Art Gallery of Ballarat, Ballarat.

Tiziano Vecello (Titian). *Tarquin and Lucretia.* 1571. Oil on canvas. Fitzwilliam Museum, Cambridge.

Van Gogh, Vincent. *Vase with Twelve Sunflowers.* 1888 or 1889. Oil on canvas. Philadelphia Museum of Art, Philadelphia.

da Vinci, Leonardo. *Scapigliata.* c. 1508. Oil on panel. *Galleria Nazionale*, Parma. 2012. *Galleria Nazionale.*

Acknowledgements

I pay my respects to the traditional owners of the lands where this novel is set: the Nukunu people of the Southern Flinders Ranges and the Kaurna people of the Adelaide Plains.

I am very grateful that this novel won the 2018 Adelaide Festival Awards for Literature Arts South Australia Wakefield Press Unpublished Manuscript Award. My thanks to the South Australian Government, Arts South Australia and Wakefield Press for their support of the award.

This book has taken years to grow. Many people have helped and encouraged me along the way. These include B.J. Amber, Wendi Avery, Anne Deveson, Sheila Duncan, Pat Hastwell, Penny Kaempf, Laine Langridge, Miriel Lenore, Gail Mahon, Kate Stewart-Moore, Kate Walsh and Mary Yeates. Dr Christian Cumming and Teresa Prior assisted me with their expertise in caring for the terminally ill.

An earlier version of this manuscript was part of my PhD thesis in creative writing at Flinders University. I am grateful to Jeri Kroll who has been an extraordinary teacher and PhD supervisor. My thanks also to my co-supervisors, Danielle Clode, Jill Golden and Rick Hosking, and to Debra Adelaide for her wonderful mentorship provided by Flinders University. To all my university colleagues I extend my thanks, especially to Sharon Kernot, Gay Lynch, Michele McCrea and Margaret Merrilees.

I thank Margot Lloyd at Wakefield Press for her brilliant editing.

I am grateful to my parents Irene and Edgar, born a century ago this year, for giving me a childhood rich in stories and songs. And to Kaz Eaton for an infinite number of things.

Wakefield Press is an independent publishing and
distribution company based in Adelaide, South Australia.
We love good stories and publish beautiful books.
To see our full range of books, please visit our website at
www.wakefieldpress.com.au
where all titles are available for purchase.
To keep up with our latest releases, news and events,
subscribe to our monthly newsletter.

Find us!

Facebook: www.facebook.com/wakefield.press
Twitter: www.twitter.com/wakefieldpress
Instagram: www.instagram.com/wakefieldpress

www.ingramcontent.com/pod-product-compliance
Lightning Source LLC
Chambersburg PA
CBHW020641260626
47157CB00008B/2858